Maria

By

John Mazur

DORRANCE
PUBLISHING CO
EST. 1920
PITTSBURGH, PENNSYLVANIA 15230

Dorrance Publishing Co
585 Alpha Drive
Suite 103
Pittsburgh, PA 15238
Visit our website at www.dorrancebookstore.com

ISBN: 979-8-8860-4665-6
eISBN: 979-8-8860-4749-3

Dedication

Tossed Emotion

I kiss'd you once, restful calamity,
Sweetest warmth, unmatch'd singularity.
Heaven's twist so complete it captivates
Total abandon, saturates reckless;
Its promise churning, agonizing bliss.

One kiss all structure gone how sweet is it.
Stunned, bewilder'd could not believe that
Somewhere way before we were mystery;
Yet cannot sing our song so happily
Till heartbeats match sweet echo's destiny.*

Delicate lips soft press, touch exquisite.
Unwoven recall never be forgot;
Undone am I, lost, all senses silken,
Mystifying, luring, no illusion:
To hold your hand still storm-toss'd emotion.

Yet senses impress sweetest rarity
As we immerse each curiosity

Contents

Chapter One

Friendship Honoring Friendship

St. Constance was a small Catholic church situated in the beautifully wooded pastoral community on the northwestern outskirts of Zakopane, Poland. It was here that our Bulgarian folk group was to perform. Quite unusual it was, for we had become accustomed to performing in larger communities and cities, performing for dignitaries, chancellors, and presidents; afterwards meeting them, shaking their hand; not uncommon to find ourselves sharing the same table; the same food and drink and sometimes, but rarely, sitting across the table from our honored dignitaries; but more likely, somewhere in the same room. Having toured throughout Europe, you might say that over the summers we had grown accustomed being received as mini dignitaries ourselves, emissaries of good will from Sofia, Bulgaria. Wherever we went we were very well accepted, and our group was quite sociable, meeting again and again with acquaintances who, over the years, had now become our friends. However, this little Catholic church was an exception beyond our scope.

Before our dance presentation, the coordinators and the people of the small parish were very helpful in getting us anything we needed. It was just a simple community festival, a summer parish church party that, over the years, had become a designation for tourist, especially of Polish heritage from the United States. No saints day needed for this celebration, just the natural surroundings of this beautiful, hidden resort town in the Tatra Mountains of

1

southern Poland. It was something the parishioners did every year to help raise money for the church and budget for short covering during the school year. There were rides and, of course, "Bingo" in the large parish hall downstairs in the basement gathering room, next to the adjoining kitchen with all its facilities. You see, this was the cafeteria for the parish high school. Grade schoolers were up on the third floor and usually either went home for lunch or stayed in school and ate at their desks; afterwards, they occupied the gymnasium, running off excess energy before afternoon classes. Whenever the weather permitted, they recessed outside. It was all nice and tidy; teachers and parents with children constantly at the peak of the triangle, no matter which way it was turned; always were the little darling accountable to both well informed parents and teachers, as any good God-fearing elementary democracy ought to be.

Later this evening, our group was to perform, actually early evening about eight o'clock, and then a nice sit-down supper of traditional Polish cooking. Our performing area was outdoors on an oaken floor laid out special for dancing and such occasions as ours; the dancing area was sizeable and more than adequate. Seeing that we were invited guest, we were treated with politeness and interest. The biggest surprise was that we had this beautiful dance floor on which to perform, half expecting the ground instead. As we were getting into our costumes, our director finally told us that our performance was a special favor we were doing for one of his old political friends, who, at one time, was heavily involved in helping the Polish people in its fight for freedom from Russia. Our director, Anton Kirkov, was also involved in undercover work with his friend who, more than once, had saved his life.

"What does your friend do now?" I asked.

"He's pastor of this parish."

Hearing this, we were all charged; we, too, hated the Russian Communist; stories of armed brutality, documentation, still fresh on our minds of how families, relatives and friends were rounded up, many shot, massacred as their armies enslaved a peaceful country that was ravished and desperate to reorganize after the brutalization of WWII. Charged to know that our director played a part in helping Poland free itself from this evil "ism," our performance this evening was outstanding in honor of him and the parish pastor, the scholarly Father, Sylvester Wronka, whom we had just met as we were warming up before our appearance. He came in to wish us good luck and not to forget "to break a leg." I had this prickly feeling that we were surrounded with hidden talent; nothing pompous or vulgar in expression but truly humble; encircled were we, emerging in this beautiful culture of which we were now a part; how wonderful that mankind is working together; cultures and nationalities coming together to celebrate life and love of life. How simple and how good is that.

Our troupe was exhilarated, expressing authentic Bulgarian folklore; individual performers were outstanding. I was especially proud of my stag leaps; they seemed to be just a little bit higher than usual and my pirouettes graceful and masculine; my chaînés turns were quick, clean and filled with pride. The Cossack coffee grinder energetic and stimulating; but my cabrioles were outstanding; instead of the quick double beats, twice in succession I beat my calves three times; that was outstanding for anyone and nearly impossible to do, and the audience really appreciated my efforts. Our singing gave us a bit of a rest; and to our surprise the audience, over a thousand strong of friends, relatives and tourists, joined in. Truly, they appreciated us; they loved us! And we loved them for loving us. Beaming with flushed cheeks, taking our bows, it was obvious that we, also, loved ourselves; our shirts wet with the sweet scent of excitement from our spirited activity. Tireless, we were, so charged; we were ready to perform again.

Off stage we walked about and mingled, standing on the side, smiling and talking, accepting congratulations and listening to one of the local Góra troupe sing and play their traditional songs; songs and dances of these mountain folks our very generous hosts. How very different were their costumes leggings and dresses compared to those Polish clans from the plain's country, up north, out East away from the Tatra Mountains.

Clans, the original families and communities of the world, remind us from whence we all came; still protective of their customs, food, music and dances, virtues and cultural morality. Feeling so proud of my Bulgarian background, I love sharing in this wonderful world of diverse, refined taste exchange of entertainment. Little by little breaking down barriers to realize how fragile, yet how wonderful are individual human difference; yet how all the same we are in wanting to be free, to do and to express ourselves to accomplish. Proof is how the great cultures merged and technologies of our marvelous civilizations grew, and so today reflect their long-ago past beginnings in the simple work-a-day ethic; their celebratory delights of music, song, and dance, never to forget good food and good Schnapps. What's left to refine is our soul, and how many times and again have we failed. So, what has changed?

In this setting of beautiful tall pines, burgeoning oaks and elms have been here longer than anyone wants to recall or to search fauna and faun genealogies. What a setting, and how appropriate for this festival; now the sun sets our stage for a softer evening of gaming and dancing. Our troupe had already separated, socializing and meandering, meeting new folds and making new acquaintances. I found myself walking with three lovely girls, who made me feel just marvelous with all their praise of my talents, but when they saw their other friends and boyfriends, politely excused themselves, and alone was I once more.

Following the entertainment crowd, I realized that we were to eat downstairs in the school cafeteria where a special meal and goodies were prepared. There were long tables obvious for the grade schoolers; also, in another area a combination of shorter tables and chairs for high school and/or faculty.

The buffet presentation was aromatically sensuous, so I quickly moved to the end of the line, taking a glass of lemonade, desperately needing to refresh myself and made my way to a table. When I pulled out my chair, I was surprised to find three lovely young ladies; each moving to stand behind his chair, vying and grinning, as if each were presenting a fresh homemade apple pie in competition for me to judge, pleased to sit next to me. Not only was I shocked, I was definitely delighted as punch or milk or coffee, whichever goes best with homemade apple pie, for each lady was a separate delight; an agreeable pleasure, whose company immediately I knew I was going to enjoy, but my surprise was that I had no idea who or how much. They had soft drinks. I believe they were homemade honey beverages of some sort, as everything at this festival was homemade.

Chapter Two

Love Happens

An exchange of names was in order. The young lady on my right had lovely natural red hair, I believe; blue eyes and a few, imperceptible, darling freckles on white cheeks. More reserved, yet, subtly, tilted her head, hello. To my left a strawberry blonde, buoyant, with a delightful turned-up nose, Pricilla Nugent, from New York City. Directly across from me was Donna Rae Gruenwald from Chicago. Hers was a smooth, tanned complexion with lovely jet-black hair; Donna Rae expressed beautiful, deep, sea green eyes; they were luminous, aglow, like her personality.

"I'm Andrei Ivanov; before I forget, you are all more than quite attractive, you are all exceptionally attractive. And I have to gather my senses about me. Oh, yes, I'm a little flustered." I began to laugh at my own awkwardness; the girls joined in, for what I said was absolutely true.

"Let's see," nervously I continued, "I'm Andrei Ivanov from Bulgaria, and I'm with the Bulgarian dance troupe."

"We know," they answered in unison, nodding, giggling together as if they rehearsed their lines and again enthusiastically responded in disjointed sequence: "We watched your performance and your solos."

Donna Rae raved: "Yes, we did; you're a marvelous dancer! Never have I seen anyone dance like that."

"However do you jump so high?" asked Pricilla, her brown eyes buzzing alive; "it's like you had wings, and for a moment you looked as if you were suspended in thin air."

"Thank you very much. You see, I work very hard to achieve that suspension; always I strive to be the best I can be."

"Definitely, you're the best in the troupe," exclaimed Donna Rae. "Oh, my, we're all talking a mile a minute; excuse us, please, this is Maria. Now, if you want fabulous, someone who is extremely talented with a brilliant mind and memory, someone like that is Maria."

"Hi," she smiled.

Instantly, in another world lost, I was helpless. I cannot even begin to describe her; but, yes, I can; she was gorgeous from top to bottom and from the way she smiled at me, she was sentient, beautiful from the inside too; she was just all there; and it all began with her right here. A strange prickly, tingly feeling came over me. Nothing was going to be the same again, I just knew it somehow. Everything about her was natural, including her unbelievable red hair, so silky that I could not take my eyes away. So I asked if I could touch her hair because I've never seen hair like this before. "Um-hum," and she leaned toward me. "Oh, my, this is like silk, this is silk!" Immediately, I apologized for my boldness, but I could not help myself.

When one is being introduced, talking about this and that, one does not muse on characteristics, unless he or she does something silly, upstaging, or stupid. And if the other person is polite that notes one to stop, to find an excuse to stay a little longer to converse; if the line is short, as is now, then it's one-on-one. For sure that takes time; and if he or she is receptive that time may lead to a date, enjoyment, figuring things out, making connections: intellectual, emotional, romantic. For who makes such connections, silently I mused; yet, I know this happens daily or nightly. Hello and goodbye is often all in one bedtime chat, both wondering just what happened, vowing never to make such a mistake again. But this was unique because I was participating in a fairytale with my own personal court: three really lovely ladies; and the one to my right was a princess. How did I manage this! Seeing that all three were Americans, my correct thoughts ought to be how lucky can one guy get! Yet, I conformed and took it all in stride, holding my emotions together, quickly suggesting that I was hungry.

"Oh, so are we," Pricilla volunteered, rising from her chair; energetically,

Donna Rae joining her. Maria just beginning to gather her purse from her lap gave me the necessary time to move behind her chair and to assist her as she rose. My attention was right; she smiled back and whispered thank you. Definitely, there was a bond; if anything, at least toward genuine politeness. I just felt so good inside; so good all over.

Food preparation was done by the parishioners, male and female cooperation, and was it good, delicious! Polish kielbasa, kraut and the cabbage rolls. The bread is truly fabulous; and it only takes one slice to believe it. For exhausted and excited dancers, it was a marvelous combination of food and drink nourishment. Tables were being filled, and many in our troupe were mingling and talking to everyone beyond themselves; casual conversation was so easy that we felt at home. People complimented us and our surprising Mazowsze encore, expressing true Polish folklore. We left our mark.

While moving in the cafeteria line, Maria turned to me to say in a quiet voice that she didn't believe that they were to be in here. "This was strictly for performers, true?"

"But you are a guest of the performers, and everyone here knows that you are part of the troupe, right?" I winked. Only to be upstaged by one of the serving ladies replenishing a milk pitcher for those who preferred milk with their coffee or just a glass of milk.

"Maria!"

"Yetta!"

"Oh, my dear, how are you; you look wonderful; how's your mother and your father, your sister? You're staying with Aunty Marsha, I believe, no?"

"Yes, I am staying with Aunty Marsha; the family is home in Chicago and plans to come next year to stay with Aunty for the summer."

"Lovely! And how long will you be staying?"

"I'm leaving tomorrow on the seven-o'clock flight to London then back to Chicago. I'm here with my two college girlfriends; this is our sixth day. I wanted to show them the town and the festival before we left."

"Are they having a good time?"

"Oh, yes, they are; oh, excuse me, Yetta, these are my good friends from college, Donna Rae from Chicago and Pricilla, New York. And this is, Andrei Ivanov, the lead dancer with the troupe from Bulgaria."

"Oh, yes, yes, we are all aware of your performance. Father Wronka told us to stop preparations and go see the wonderful dancers from Bulgaria," looking with admiration at Andrei, doubtless admiring his dancer's physique. "I saw all of it, you know. You are quite good; very good, if I do say so. Your group just kept the audience attention so wonderfully; they were caught up, not expecting your beautiful Mazowsze singing. Why you had some of us in tears; did you know that? Some of the older folks were crying?"

"We did notice and thank you, thank you very much."

"Well, don't let your food get cold now, my darlings. It's always best when it's hot. Nice meeting you, Andrei."

Yetta continued moving alongside Andrei, telling him what was better and best to eat. "And Andrei," she emphasized, "you must get to know a great Zakopane surprise of our own. Do get acquainted with our Maria."

Maria and the two girls were already moving toward our table when Yetta reached for my arm again. "After dinner, ask Maria to play for you; there's a piano in the rehearsal room behind the kitchen here. Just go down this hall," pointing toward the hallway, "through that back door; continue on and through the second door, only door," she laughed, "and you will be on the back stage. She knows where it is; no one's in there now, so you won't be disturbed. Have her play for you."

Amid all this wonderful music, song and dance, with beautiful, young marriageable women and handsome available men, was in some ways, displaying the imaginable ecstasies of yesteryear's good harvest, instigating a good chase for a good wife and/or husband; sometimes it was danced and sung in counterpoint with the beautiful young maids in charge doing the plotting and hunting, displaying feats of graceful feminine agility, cleverly outdoing the men who joyously out did themselves in masculine prowess for their favorite maid; their dance choreography done in dazzling speed and precision in time with the spirited music required great strength. Abundant femininity was quite obvious and robust in timely parallel complementary movement of which some was modestly robust, with teasing gestures and playful attitudes, expressing the dance of boy-girl, girl-boy romantic courting.

Traditional songs and dances celebrated the grain harvest with its abundance and prosperity, predicting good fortune, foretelling marriages within the year. Such glorious movement reflected the balance of nature and the preferential nature of loving humanity, man and woman working together.

Masculinity's strength, dynamic leaps and jumps, feats of unbelievable athletic and heroic prowess, balanced with complementary gracefulness of the young ladies' feminine and surprising tempestuous movements; endeavors in which the audience was overwhelmed, mesmerized. Enticing feminine smiles and the dexterity of their dancing somehow was to hint of her marvelous baking skills, all in promise and subtlety displayed through the movement of her skirt, her smile, and the tilt of her head, her voice in song, and the creativity of her lost and found handkerchief. Elegant, fluid in the manner of courtly tradition; poised forever were these reflections in every romantic heart gracefully relived of an era gone.

It became an Old Testament audience wrapped in emotions of their past, their deeds, their loves and losses; most began to sing along with the performers, smiling joyous; others tearing, crying for the memories of their often repeated nighttime stories now remembered by parents and grandparents of a past that was warm and sad. A moving sight it was, recalling spontaneous memories of humanity now and forever its best.

Definitely every culture is unique; some things are close, but there is always that difference that makes it special, unique, and this Polish food was superb; and there rye bread, truly the staff of life. I told the girls that there was an old Jewish proverb that said every Jew must buy his bread from the Jewish bread maker, but if the Jewish bread maker is not good, the Jew is exempt and can buy his loaf from the gentile down the street.

"Always exemptions," answered Maria.

"And that's part of the excitement of life," Donna Rae added.

"How true is that? Why, if we all had to adhere to the rules, we'd all be bored," smiled Pricilla.

"For sure, dead from hunger," I added.

Silence about the table as we all cut and took hardy bites of our food, enjoying its flavors with hums and murmurs, coinciding praiseworthy nods of obvious approval.

"I heard that you play the piano; that there's a stage down that hall through the second door. Yetta said that you know the way. Is it true?"

Maria stopped, astonished that Andrei would know this; then recalled Yetta talking to him. Gathering her composure, softly she answered: "Yes, there is a small rehearsal and performance stage behind the second door."

"Oh, Andrei, you've got to hear her play before you go," Pricilla frankly excited that someone would like to hear her friend play.

"She's terrific," said Donna Rae, her sea green eyes shining enthusiasm at the thought of hearing her best friend play for someone other than her coach.

"Well, I haven't played for a while," Maria spoke up.

"You played yesterday for over four hours," Pricilla reminded her. Maria, wishing she could hide while her lightly freckled cheeks tinged pink. "Aunty Marsha took us to town and to lunch; we even visited a few old wooden churches in the area while you were at home rehearsing. Surely, you haven't forgotten."

"When we returned," Donna Rae continued, almost in rapid fire, "it was after one P.M.; you had a bite at the house, and we felt bad that you didn't join us, so we went back out and had dinner atop the mountain, with the fading sun behind the peaks, it was a to-die-for scene; so romantic as the town beneath us slowly came alive, turning on its lights one by one, calling us to the Polish pubs and their lively nightlife. Fun and a lot of crazy guys from all over the world; not really romantic; well, your aunt and your uncle, Walter, were there, but he wasn't our type, although he's really nice. I like his blue eyes," Donna Rae, letting the manhunt out of her bag while Pricilla acknowledged her types and colors:

"I like his fabulous, natural creamy complexion; I've never seen a guy his age in such vigorous shape with such rosy cheeks. Maria, this is our sixth night here, and we're sad at leaving tomorrow. And Andrei's never heard you play, who knows, you may never see him again. You are your own agenda, you know; it's quite demanding. Come on, play for us; just once let the cat out of the bag; you know the big grand ebony one that sits on three legs and is seven feet tall, even when he's lying down."

"Come on, break your rule," Donna Rae putting her hand to her mouth as if the slip would go unnoticed.

"What rule was that?" I asked.

"Well," Donna Rae revealed, "she was told by her instructor not to play for just anyone because they just wouldn't appreciate what she does: her time, her effort and long hours of practice. The ordinary person just doesn't under-stand; she's to play for audiences only, paying ones at that."

"Well, I can't afford to pay to hear you, but I guarantee you, I'm not like the ordinary guy. I love jazz. I love piano music; Chopin's my favorite, my favorite composer; I never tire of listening to his music. He's in a class entirely by himself."

Exhilarated, Donna Rae and Pricilla beamed like quartz iodine headlights, looking at Maria.

"His favorite classical composer is Chopin; isn't that wild, Maria," Donna Rae raved, taking a sip of her delicious raspberry shake made with real Zakopane garden raspberries.

"Yeah, coincidence or not; it's a sign, Maria," Pricilla added, her voice animated, pleased that her buddy, Maria, was going to play for a guy, a real guy at that.

"And I'm sure Yetta told you, as you were leaving the food line; I can't believe she mentioned it," Maria answered with a slight smile of feigned indulgence.

"Maria," I said, "Yetta did tell me that I was to ask you to play for me, but if you don't want to, it's okay. I understand. She should not have said anything, yet for her to say such a thing means, to me, as I see it, she's very proud of you; if I may extend her comment, I believe most everyone in this parish is proud of you. So there, you have my take; you don't have to play for me; I'll just always wonder. And if one day I get a chance, I'll pay for the privilege to hear you."

Warmed with approval, Maria gleamed, thinking how silly was she being, slightly disdainful toward sincere feelings; honestly, she liked the young Bulgaria dancer. He was talented, for sure, not obnoxious but graceful in manner and manners; masculine in appearance, definitely, quite handsome. While logic was giving sway to emerging emotional confirmation, Maria confided earlier to her inner self that she felt drawn to Andrei when watching his performance, marveling at his agility, his gracefulness, and his smile, long before she found herself walking down the hall with him, nonchalantly, conversing; then having him sit to her left as the fourth person at their table. It was all very unusual yet comforting. Naturally, one thing was leading to another. Never before had she played for any date or acquaintance, keeping all her performing talents for her instructor's criticism and advice. For herself, alone, she was ruthless in her discipline. A very good habit that she had developed quite naturally since childhood; a good habit that she enjoyed immensely, for every time she practiced,

11

she improved; that made her very protective, secretive of her talent, sometimes inwardly smug. It was not a talent to flaunt because, as her instructor admonished, it was not yet ready; but it and she were very close at hand. Yes, it was a silly pun, but he was clever to say it as a reminder to keep her from revealing her piano abilities too soon; actually, he wanted to be her coach and agent for next year's European debut. And this no one knew but the two of them. However, he wasn't around now, and he would never know. Because the way she felt for Andrei was so unusual that Maria was finding it natural to play something for him; besides, he was a fellow artist whose favorite piano composer happens to be Chopin, her inner voice applauded. So she told him that her forte was Chopin; and how did he know Chopin was her favorite composer. In being coy, Maria surmised that it was Yetta, "the little home ruler," who told him so. Instead, he looked at her expressionless; honestly, reiterating that he loved Chopin's waltzes, his stately Polonaises, Etudes, and his romantic Preludes, especially the wonderfully romantic one in A Major, Opus 29.

"These were wonderful compositions to dance to; their musical chording, phrasing that ignited added adrenaline into the hearts of its dancers, so that their performance was inborn, comprised within tradition, an inherited arrogance embedded within the soil of Poland. When dancing to this music, one felt inherently marvelous, important, and aristocratic."

"You seem to know a good deal about our feelings."

"Maria, I'm Bulgarian; a folk dancer. I know about the music of character, and the people who perform it. We are one; besides, Sofija is only nine hundred kilometers from Zakopane."

Admiring his gentle insistence, Maria chuckled to herself, smiling fondly: "That's about four hundred and sixty miles in the United States; like going from Chicago Minneapolis, Minnesota, by car."

*   *   *

Conversation continued between my two friends and Andrei, our new acquaintance. It was light banter: about what they had in common; interesting how we all met; who would have supposed and so on. Pleasantly inquisitive, Andrei wanted to know everything about everyone.

While the three of them conversed, it gave me time to observe and minimally participate, while nibbling my delicious strudel and sipping my coffee, again thinking should I or should I not play.

That I play for a complete stranger was quite an absurd thought. I played for instructors all the time; some sit and listen, criticize, correct and make suggestions; others just judge. This last semester when I played for the Juilliard audience everyone listened and enjoyed my playing, even when it wasn't Chopin. Not surprising to few who knew me that I so enjoyed good piano jazz like Lynne Arriale's piano and her trio, wonderfully intuitive.

She's really good; strong where she has to be, almost as strong a man's hand; then, again, marvelously soft, delicate, tenderly crawling into the personal corners of one's soul in the wee hours of the morning where hide all lost feelings of unrequited love; relationships that never matured, in spite of all their promise; or regret for something not quite accomplished, or just feeling sad over nothing—feeling sad to feel sad: maybe a little rebellion or simply moody, sorry for oneself, myself. Realizing that neither have I the time for such show of affection's extravagance, nor the time to rehearse that whimsical new schedule's run, so, dutifully, I awake.

Her rendition of Bess, You Is My Woman Now is so sensitive, so proud, so deeply moving; sad, yet true; beautifully moving to the emotions, recalling every young couple's joy and fear. But through such sadness life continues we are told; then sometimes, no matter how often we are told to straighten out and move ahead, we just falter and fall away. Call it weakness; call it loss; really, it's loss of soul; loss of caring, the true guardian of one's passion and virtue for loving; that takes real reckoning. Sometimes God, if one can find him, needs to shake you up, to give you hope again; bottom line: rebirth in confidence, self-esteem. That's reawakening!

I'm twenty-one and my life has always been the classics, with minor dalliances here and there. I do so love Chopin, yet there are so few who play him well. Now the field is wide open again, and I'm rising, getting ready for the opportune moment when I will take center stage. Believe me; I can see it; taste it. So far it's been a magnificent journey, and Mother says it's only going to get better. My teachers at Juilliard agree, but Mother knows best.

Now there's this lead Bulgarian dancer, Andrei Ivanov, asking me to play. But he hasn't any idea what I'll play; no idea, although Donna Rae and Pricilla, hopeless romantics that they are, will insist on Chopin, now that they know he's also Andrei's favorite composer. For politeness, he'll probably sit and endure; then tell me he loves it and loves me. So what else is new? Am I that easy? Is my heart so visible on my sleeve? Also, I'm not waiting for Chopin to reappear; then, again, I wouldn't mind. For I would write down all those melodies he ignored or simply forgot while in the passion of spontaneous improvisation, for he was of weak health, of frail constitution, especially toward the end of his young life, dying at thirty-nine. No, I'm not waiting for him; the age difference would be dramatic, gigantic, she began laughing to herself. However, if God willed it, he'd be just a few years older than I, or, perhaps, a few years younger; either way is perfect!

*   *   *

"Your friends here say that you play Chopin very well. Is this true?"

"Yes, it's true; I'm guilty. But I play other things too."

"Maria, stop! Please stop! Who doesn't love Chopin? I could listen to him all day."

"You can?" I do admit, I enjoyed watching him wiggle pleasure in his chair; his hands expressive in hopeful anticipation.

"My God, yes, yes; I'm thrilled that you will play; if you're not too tired, I'd love to hear you. Yetta told me the rehearsal stage is empty, so we will not be disturbed. I figure, it will be quiet, and you may play anything you want; of course, I know it will be wonderful, and no one will know anything, but do make it Chopin; that is, if you don't mind."

Everything turned on a dime; my thoughts reeling; my composure weakening; smiling to myself, I no longer could hold off, so I smiled at him and nodded okay, pleased that not only did Andrei like Chopin, but also, I liked his positive, continued, gentle determination. I confess, now, I felt tingly and guilty inside for thinking such mean thoughts, for it was always those in the music world at Juilliard who loved to hear me play; but it was their business to develop me. Andrei, here, was just an ordinary guy from Sofija, Bulgaria, a very nice guy; and their troupe's principal dancer. Then again, he's European and probably has less than the usual rock-'n-roll, rhythm-and-blues agenda of his friends. I wonder how old he is. He's eyes are alight. He's happy and that makes me happy too.

Chapter Three

Where Do I Sign

We left the noisy conversation-filled cafeteria, and started down the hall. Donna Rae opened the first door, and Pricilla eagerly moved ahead of us to open the second. I detected excitement not just from me but from my two friends. They were charged, faces flushed, that I was going to play for a guy, and that guy made everything more interesting; for I detected that he, too, was just as excited but more so, though he knew not that he was being led into the inner chamber of a musician's heart—his rehearsal room; in this instance, a very small stage. Nevertheless, a very private inner chamber of the meditative soul, few people ever get to see, let alone explore. One stage work light was on, centering on a highly polished grand Bosendorfer. Pricilla and Donna Rae raised the heavy lid of the deep mahogany, almost black, seven-foot cat; Andrei then held it, marveling at its size and beauty, while Pricilla raised the support stick; slowly, gently, so not to damage anything, Andrei settled it back on its support. Donna Rae then removed the music holder.

"Why is she removing that?" Andrei asked Pricilla.

"It's preparing the piano for a concert and its full sound. Maria doesn't need any music, she has fabulous recall; anyway when playing a concert, it's all from memory; no music allowed. She also has two majors, the second is Biology. Fabulous memory, nothing escapes her."

Now very charged, my two buddies found their seats in the little auditorium.

Instead of Andrei Ivanov sitting with them, to my surprise, he found a chair and sat to the right of my piano bench. An unexpected move, nevertheless, I was excited; impulsively, I felt like playing Chopin's GRANDE VALSE BRIL-LIANTE; you know the one in E flat major, OPUS 18. But no way was I going to jump into that romantic heartbeat; being the pro that I was taught to be, more like preparing to be, I began simply; warming up my eager fingers that hadn't played since early morning's pre-breakfast and then after. More and more, I was beginning to like this guy; and I sensed that he liked me too; he was different: a doer; intellectually inquisitive, mentally strong and, yes, a gen-uine goodness; undeniably, again, physically appealing; yet he was sensitive, secure and sure of himself in a quiet unassuming way. There was no pretense, no airs. I had had boyfriends before but nothing ever materialized beyond "hello, how are you" and maybe a date. But I confess, and I know it sounds to-tally immature, this guy, sitting next to me, was becoming a heartthrob, my first, although he never knew it.

I just had to control myself; not that I would throw myself at him, but that I might say something stupid. While continuing to warm up, he just watched in silence; but nothing was to fluster my playing to make me look bad or sound ridiculous. Quietly, he pulled up his folding chair a little closer to my bench then respectfully asked if there was anything that he might do for me, or anything that I might need. "No, thank you," I answered as I continued to chord familiar and favorite Chopinic phrases, moving up and down the key-board listening; not surprising, the grand cat was in tune; I now continued with runs up and down, loosening, stretching my fingers, warming my shoul-ders and arm muscles. During the exercise on the beautiful seven-foot open grand, I asked, again, satisfying my curiosity, teasing the attractive one, pa-tiently sitting in his chair next to me.

"So, you truly like Chopin?"

"Who doesn't," correctly, he anxiously replied again. "I can listen to him all day; that is, on DVDs and once at an amateur concert in high school, but never, ever this close; so personal and so private, sitting next to the musi-cian herself. It's all so special, Maria."

His enthusiasm was genuine; smiling, I knew we were both pleased, on the same page. A quick glance at my two girlfriends who were only seated a few rows away, looking directly at the keyboard of the piano on the simple

16

two-foot-elevated stage. They were situated perfectly to watch my hands.

"This is mind-blowing," Pricilla quickly whispered to Donna Rae.

"It certainly is something."

"I bet you a homemade raspberry slush that she gives him a private concert; that's more than three compositions. Are you on?"

"Yeah," said Donna Rae. "And from the way she's been looking at him, you may be right."

"I know I'm right, shake?"

"You bet!"

Suddenly everything was quiet in the tiny hall.

Closing her eyes to composed body and soul, Maria sat motionless. A few moments later, she stepped into her world, so loving embraced the keyboard before her. So patient, the man sitting to her right would now hear a live performance of Chopin's MAZURKA, IN C-SHARP MINOR, OPUS 63.

Childlike she began, softly; slowly increasing intensity, left hand embellishing the right hand's simple melody; playful, yet unpretentious in delicate shading; the piece continued to develop into a graceful, stately Mazurka for only two lovers. Right then, I realized that I was listening to someone's soul; yes, Chopin's composition, but it was Maria's soul. Never had I expected to hear anything so beautiful; so accomplished; so exquisitely played, full of emotion: chords, musical phrases, smiling, teasing joy of its lover's dance. Before I had time to consider what I had just witnessed, Maria followed with the MAZURKA IN B-FLAT, OPUS 7.

Dramatic, yet under complete control; in six-eight time keys ring, summoning temptation to the dance; couples rushing onto the floor, subtly winking to one's partner; expressive thoughts, playful pauses to enhance expressions, sensations of deeper love for one another; arm in arm through graceful movements, embracing melodies fully poetic, musically alluring, every chord promising romance. With sweetest aristocratic character, truly Polish; proud is the lyrical society that still thrives in its own country; a country, whose people for generations have bravely fought for, died for; and now, joyful of life as is their generous nature so full of freedom. I was hearing Chopin played just as he felt it, capturing that inborn, indigenous God-given human spirit that originates within the soul of a people that live forever. I was genuinely amazed, truly. Maria's playing was magnificent, so full of feeling that I began to tear, thinking how close to home I was.

"Brava, Brava, magnificent!"

"Oh, don't stop!" Pricilla and Donna Rae raved, loving to hear their friend play, who for years now were her favorite audience.

Turning to me, gently leaning, Maria gently asked, so not to break the mood, "What would Andrei like to have me play?"

Bewitched, totally caught off guard. Why, I imagine she could play anything in the whole world, yet she asked me for my referral.

"It's all so marvelous, please continue; now you know that Chopin's my favorite piano composer; definitely, you are my preferred Chopin pianist."

"You certainly know the right thing to say to a girl."

"And you certainly know how to woo a guy."

"Please, Andrei, I'm not wooing any guy; though understand you're not just any guy. Besides my instructor, you're the first man I've enjoyed ever playing for; you don't correct or admonish me. You simply enjoy my playing."

"Indeed I do. Do you know that you are quite beautiful?" Maria blushed fully, her blue eyes ignited, totally caught off guard. "And I'm beginning to realize that never shall I know how complicated you really are."

"You are a charmer," Maria countered, quickly trying to recover from a total broadside; still blushing, continuing to reclaim her thoughts; to restore poetic balance yet not completely able to adjust to Andrei's previous comment, noting to herself that no one has ever said that she was "quite beautiful."

"Thank you for that lovely compliment; I'm quite simple, you know," shaking her head indifference but aglow with his compliment. "But you must bear in mind, it's the music, and we're not to get carried away. I'll play whatever you request; if I don't know it, just hum it, and I'll play it."

"Let it be more Chopin, please."

They smiled at one another, while Maria's two buddies remained quiet, watching the episode determined to unfold.

Suddenly, something feverish within her told her he's the one, and just as quickly she was overcome with feelings of inspiration. "Andrei, I am going to play for you a few pieces that I have been perfecting for my next year's debut concert in Vienna; that is if you don't mind?"

Under her spell, Andrei just nodded and smiled, whispering, "Yes, please," pinching himself for such unexpected reality.

Maria turned back to the keyboard. When she did he noticed something unique about her, but he couldn't place it or figure it out. His interest in anthropology came to the fore, knocking. Yes, that's it, he thought to himself; she a true Celt an authentic rarity: eyes bluer than the sky; her hair definitely red, which, perhaps, one day may turn auburn; and lips, natural-luxurious— the soft blush of early morning light, waking young rosebuds. A true descendent of Ireland, Wales; maybe she can even trace her heritage to some of the pre-Roman inhabitants of Britain, Gaul; or possibly a little later. Perhaps her family was associated with the Court of King Arthur where she was the beautiful Elaine, who hopelessly fell in love with Lancelot and later died of unrequited love. Definitely, most certainly, she's a muse, not an abstraction, though clearly meditative.

"Andrei, Andrei," softly Maria summoned him back from the Isle of Avalon. "Is there something wrong; you look as if you're far away?"

"I was; but I'm back. To be honest I was trying to make out your heritage."

"And you thought?"

"You are Irish; but you are Polish, I believe?"

"But my mother told me that my great-grandfather was Irish, and red hair is not uncommon in our family tree. But we can talk about that mundane topic later."

"I'm sorry. I broke your concentration."

"Not to worry," she smiled, "I can get it under control again, especially for someone who loves Chopin. I believe you're familiar with this heroic piece. It was composed to help bolster the spirit of the Polish people in their battle against Russia's suppressive invasion in 1830, ending sadly in defeat in September 1831."

Separating from their little conversation, Maria, with a grand, rosy smile, again, focused herself. Instantly, thunderous images, of THE REVOLUTION flashed colors, military uniforms; explosives' residue filling the sky; dark, voracious gunpowder screams anger; ironies most beautiful colors setting against the sun of blood red magentas on rage; purple patches of lyrical poetry turned ugly; mingling stench; confusing lines, guns; embolden men charging, bayonets clashing, blood spouting. Inhuman effort surging to victorious confusion; cries, bodies twisted, contorted, piled, heaped one upon another dead, dying,

19

merciless pain, impeding movement. Horses are down in agony, waiting to be shot. Breathless putrid air, men gasping exhaustion; yet continuing on to a more violent end: defeat, then quiet for souls to depart.

Intense is she to behold; full of fire, determination, majestic; immersed in her own world, Maria is the last to know that she is her own revolution; and she's in a place that I may only enjoy from afar. Marriage, I thought, how silly; yet how delightful it would be to love someone so complete in her art form, however, she's in love with her first love, Chopin. And he has no idea how lucky he is.

Looking up from her world, her hands graceful; her face flushed, smiling love. Maria's rejuvenated. Eyes intense happiness; her soul a title wave, a cascading estuary, rushing romantic full bore; turning to Andrei, she whispers: "You'll love this next piece; it's one of my favorites, THE FANTASIE-IM-PROMPTU."

Her two buddies watching the show, listening to Maria's playing, were unaware that earlier a few locals had meandered into the hall and were already situated in the last rows resting or romantically inclined. Nevertheless, they too sat up and took notice of the grand performance and its surrounding activities (vigorously applauded the accomplished pianist).

"Maria's in love," Pricilla leaning her head toward Donna Rae.

"She is. I've never heard her play the FANTASIE-IMPROMPTU with such intense longing; her transitions so dramatic, so soft, such loving sweetness."

"Andrei's magic for her. Listen to that rainbow transition. How exquisite is that."

"She's letting herself go; she laying it all out for him; she's playing pieces that are part of her repertoire for her debut next year. Oh, my God, what a moment. I'm so happy for her; for them both."

"Memorable, Donna Rae, memorable moments; they deserve one another, truly they do; look at him watching her. He's totally captivated; he's caught."

"Of course, they're in love," Donna Rae clutching Pricilla's arm, joyful for her buddy. "Oh, my God, how beautiful is this."

Turning slightly to Andrei, smiling, Maria was elated. His response was amazement, looking at her as if she were the Goddess, Euterpe, and, he, caught in her web, loving every loop, every tie, every phrase, captured; watching her remarkable strong, powerful hands; adroit fingers, nimble, yet graceful; she was mesmerizing, forever beautiful. Neither said a word, but stayed more than a brief look at one another; so pleased was she with the young man next to her; not even a glance at the keyboard, enjoying one another's rapture, as she lovingly continued with the rainbow theme, recalling to how she often blind-folded herself during this particular passage, not for memory of notes and fin-gering but for its sweetness, its escape into the sky. Her musical memory recalled, Maria transitioned renewed energy into her world; and this time per-mitted Andrei entrance. Welcoming new emotions' quick transition press in-tense through her nimble fingers; conjuring a blur, rushing fantasies, fantastic over the keyboard to its glorious ending; then back, once more, softly, to their rainbow, wondrous and emotional her last soft chords tying them spiritually and lovingly together.

"It's fantasy," he gasped. "Maria, am I dreaming?"

"It's the FANTASIE-IMPROMPTU. You're allowed to dream; it's un-derstood, a given; whatever romantic fantasy your heart desires."

"I did, for sure I did, and you're simply marvelous; you're incredible."

"I see tears in your dark eyes; you must have enjoyed it."

"I did. It was you that I enjoyed; of course, your playing is without say-ing," shaking his head, choking back his emotions, moving, sensitive. "You are a rare creature as is your talent."

Here was the prelude to their rainbow of which he said she was its muse, a Goddess. In its shading, he saw every color, distinct and true from its point well above the trees, a perfect ribbon over the hills: reds, yellows, blues, violets blending courageous, slow and hopeful, as were they to remain; yet impercep-tibly, waning; liquefying, back into the honey sweetness of the sky, a reminder of how limited is our time anywhere here on Earth.

"I loved it; thank you, Maria. Truly, I'm the one chasing rainbows; I find them so emotional, and you are their muse."

"That melody was made into a very popular song: I'M ALWAYS CHAS-ING RAINBOWS by Judy Garland."

"I've heard it sung and played by Louis Armstrong, too."

"Yes, I've heard that version too. Are you acquainted with the jazz piano sounds of Lynne Arriale and her trio?"

"Not until now, thank you. I'll make a note of it."

"Miles Davis?"

"Is sugar sweet?" They exchanged warm, approving smiles.

What a lovely insight, she thought. He really does like jazz.

Remembering what he read about Chopin's introduction to Parisian society, he began to tell Maria. Although she knew the tale, she let him tell it for love of his enthusiasm, and, even more, she loved him for telling it.

"You know, we should have no lights except for the candelabra that I bring to your piano. It was how that fabulous pianist, infamous lover, Franz Liszt, the Hungarian, introduced his new friend, Chopin. It was quite dramatic, but that was Liszt with one of his best nighttime moves. At once, the society of the Paris loved their new darling, Chopin. At first, they all thought it was Liszt playing, for the entire salon was dark, and Liszt was not unaccustomed to such dramatics. (For it was somewhat discreetly whispered behind cover of the feminine fan, as tale within tale has it known throughout classical oral tradition, Liszt was so loved that at one time or another, he had known every woman in the salon intimately. France was the most Catholic country in Europe and confession was a great remission of sin—so all was forgiven.) When they saw him making his way through the darkened room with a lighted candelabra, placing it on the piano, the audience was stunned to find another pianist playing in total darkness; as time went on, Chopin's compositions they found more passionate, earthy, romantically dynamic, conjuring scenes of families, communities and lovers; a sensitive recollection of Poland that most Parisians considered strange and exotic, for few knew anything of that unusual land, outside, east of Germany. "You play these as if you were Polish."

"I am on my mother's side; she, herself, is quite an accomplished pianist; it was she who was my first teacher."

"I would love to sit next to you, to touch you."

"Why?"

"Because I feel you bring good luck to anyone who touches you before or as you play."

"And what about after I play? Will I be dull, dark and dangerous; someone to shun," she teased, watching the handsome man next to her blush bungling embarrassment.

"Oh, my God, forgive me, I'm too bold. Please, Maria, I apologize."

"You're a romantic."

"So are you to play Chopin the way you do."

"Romantics, you know, are the best kind of people: imaginative, very creative and honest. You may sit next to me, but on the very end of the bench."

"Now he's sitting on the piano bench." Pricilla nudged her buddy.

"You won the bet," whispered Donna Rae.

"I know you need the arm room, Maria."

"Indeed, I do, but first touch me. You too make me feel so good just being here next to me."

Kissing his right index finger, André gently, almost imperceptibly, touched Maria's warm now glowing left cheek as she faced him. Not moving, she felt the light intensity of his touch. After making a tiny circle, he outlined her lips then withdrew, but Maria still felt its gentle motion, delayed but not confined, beginning now to stir, tingling within her body. The feeling didn't settle in one area; it settled everywhere.

"Maria," he silently whispered, feeling gallant; doubtless it was due to her playing with such passionate underlying hints that gave him the feeling of exclusivity.

"Yes."

"May I kiss you?"

"No!" boldly, she countered; then instantly volleyed her womanly contrariety: "Please, no harm intended; it's meant to curb your romantic ambitions," she placated the handsome young man to her right. Realizing, this good-looking man who called her beautiful couldn't be all that bad, slowly letting her womanly passions take hold. Maria quite wiggled out of the situation, although managed to leave the door unlatched: "We will now imaginatively dance to the MINUTE WALTZ."

"That will only stimulate romantic ambitions."

"Be quiet!" Smiling, she winked. "Privilege has ended."

"Yes, my lady," and he complemented her movement.

The brisk MINUTE WALTZ over, Andrei did not move while Maria remained quiet, her graceful hands in her lap. Somehow, each was very near to the other; and lower lip to lip undeniably embraced. Lips were plush; each to each, strangely shy still, enticing as lips are when full in love. Again lips to lips and hands held; neither wanting to separate yet slowly separating. Maria

23

flushed, heated yet slowly she separated as did Andrei with her; yet each continued to hold the other's hand.

"Is this what it's like to truly be kissed," each feeling the warmth of the other's breadth. "Never have I felt this way before."

"Never have I, Maria, but we live in two different worlds."

"That's not our subject; it's playing I want to do for you; and I must; so let me?"

Releasing their hands, he slid back to the end of the bench. Smiling at one another, Andrei was totally tied not quite knowing what had just happened; but Maria felt quite inspired, warmth glowing throughout. Without saying anything, her feelings could not be denied. Calling for no explanation but to fulfill the inkling continuation of tinges of love's savoring emotion. Intuitively, she began the beautifully sensitive and romantic RAINDROP-PRELUDE (IN D-FLAT MAJOR, OPUS 28).

Softly, rosy cheeks of love began to play; although still flustered, for the moment, Andrei's command was her response, and he loved her every note. It was a longer piece, but Maria was ready and in control of every transition. Magical, loving fingers poetically ranged the keyboard, as was her daily occurrence. But now she had a very special audience for whom she played: the young première dancer from Bulgaria. Maria was in love; both were transported to another realm.

"I see each raindrop falling to the Earth filling up puddles, ponds, running into creeks and no way to return; but that's impossible; yet Nature has spoken, and I cry. For love whispers love, hello and goodbye."

"How poetical."

"That's because of you, here and now."

Then she led them into the valley of true love, with The PRELUDE IN A MAJOR OPUS 28-7. That simple beloved piece was the tip of their loving iceberg; melting deeper than any ocean; calling the souls of all true lovers beyond infinity. It cinched the deal. Andrei Ivanov couldn't wait to sign the papers, making Maria his Maria. Irrepressible, lips met lips once more, so eager they embraced their love, for sentient powers were at work.

"I've never heard anything like this ever. It's so rich and tender, delicate; yet full up to bursting such refine-woven human emotions. Feelings I've never experienced before. Simply sublime."

"It's all because of you."

Quietly, they sat wrapped one another's senses, silence deep and revealing. Maria looked up.

"Let's end this little music session on a brisk and higher note and then take on the evening, for I want to get to know more about you. Tomorrow morning, I must leave at seven to catch my ten-o'clock flight to America."

"Yes, better, I too would like to know you, and I have so much to learn."

"I want to play two pieces just for you; and it will complete my simple concert, so you will have some little idea of what I'm working on when you think of me."

Gaily, Maria moved right into the WALTZ no. 6 in D-Flat Major OPUS 64-1. Then with no break, she commenced the gay and flirtatious GRAND WALTZ BRILLIANTE, all the while embracing loving smiles to one another, right from its inception through its fanciful ending. Both were moving their heads in rhythmic synchronization. Definitely, they were dance partners, love partners, for this was a new Maria and her love, the enamored Andrei.

Spontaneous Maria and I passionately kissed. Just as suddenly we broke it off, but not surprised. Confused we were of what had happened and no room was at hand. So, we did the next best thing, held hands and tenderly kissed silken lips again. Donna Rae and Pricilla applauded as did a few couples, to everyone's surprise, hidden in the shadows in the back of the auditorium. We steadied ourselves, pleased with our discovery; looking into one another's eyes, smiling acknowledgment at what had taken place. I thank Maria for a fabulous performance. She squeezed my hand thank you and smiled, less nervous over what had just taken place.

"I honestly could listen to you forever, my voice trembling."

"Forever is a long time."

"But I've never felt so alive and so in love. You know what I mean?"

"Yes, yes, I do."

"And this is my memory of love, and how I will always remember you."

"And I you."

Again, surprise applause came from some few lovers somewhere in the far back row, out of sight, requesting her to play the PRELUDE IN A once more.

Whispering breathless to Andrei: "Someone has our same feelings."

25

"Perhaps, but hardly ours," we unabashedly blushed.

Once more THE PRELUDE IN A was played. Softly, I kissed her shoulder, wishing I were that blouse covering that shoulder, always to be that close. When she finished, Maria reached for my hand; quietly we sat, neither spoke, yet our world was overflowing.

"Is there a quiet place where we can go and just talk?"

"Donna Rae and Pricilla will accompany us."

"That's fine."

"That's sweet of you, my dear, but I'll think of something."

Chapter Four

The Trampolina

New to one another, new to life, so innocence ventures into the night to learn more about each other. So it is, and so it shall be.

Donna Rae and Pricilla came up to the little stage and joined compliments with Andrei of Maria's playing. Everyone very excited.

"Andrei would like to go somewhere where he and I can just talk."

"It's impossible this time of year; the town is filled, bars and restaurants jammed with tourist," emphasized Pricilla.

"What about the Truskawka Kapelusz (Strawberry Hat); fabulous salads and good sausage," Donna Rae, proud of her Polish pronunciation, really thinking of food again, although she looked like a toothpick; that is, a nicely proportioned one, if there is such a toothpick.

"Andrei wants to talk with me; he hinted that I might know a place that's dark and quiet."

"Well, do you?" Donna Rae inquired. "You used to live here, right?"

"That was just for a few weeks in the summertime when my mother and I returned to visit Aunty Marsha," Maria still sitting, turned to Andrei. Then she smiled a light.

"Where is it?" Pricilla smiled back

"For sure you three have never been there," awkwardly Maria popped out, forgetting whom she was with.

"Da-ah," Donna and Pricilla evoked the American sound of supreme intellectual finality, causing all to laugh and Andrei to state: "Even I know what that means." Instantly, everyone became more comfortable.

"We're going to the Trampolina," Maria announced.

"Where's that; what is it?" everyone asked, curiosity hovering.

"It's a place where cool people like us gather to dance, drink and eat. It's at the base of the ski lift, and the view of Zakopane is beautiful; I'll drive us there. I'll only have one drink, so you can have a good time and not worry about getting back safely."

"Why is it called the Trampolina? Is it a place for acrobats or gymnasts?" Andrei playfully cocked his head to either side.

"Are there guys there so Donna Rae and I can have a real-live male partner?"

"Plenty! And when we get there, you'll quickly understand why it's called the Trampolina."

Maria led the happy group out the back door into a little foyer, where a left-hand turn would lead into the sacristy of the church. Instead of going into the sacristy, she turned right, down a few stairs and walked outside onto the churchyard grounds that surrounded the convent. It was all very pleasant, peaceful was more like it: bushes were trimmed, grass was cut, and the flowers surrounding the two-story brick and wooden home of the nuns was calming. Especially protected were the convent walls with a large porch that surrounded three-quarters of the nunnery; their own world with inviting comfortable, small garden tables and chairs on the lawn under mature oaks and elms and some mighty savvy pines that eventually took center stage after fall's colors were spent, so our revered teaching nuns of the order of Notre Dame had the enjoyment of all the mountain seasons. Walking down the sidewalk with the sun beginning to cast its long summer shadows was very pleasant for us; our conversation was hushed and reverential. A sense of control over our destiny and direction of our lives was felt, at least, for the moment; for soon all would be forgotten at the wild Trampoline, probably as soon as we got into Maria's Pugeot.

Once squeezed in, I scooted toward the mountains, everyone jabbering. The road was in excellent condition: no one was on it. Either the party at the top was over, or everyone was having one wonderful time. On our arrival, the view from the parking lot was fantastic and more so when we all got out stretching our legs. Making our way toward the Trampolina, we were energy talking all at once, excited. Simultaneously, Andrei and I reached for each other's hand to squeezed and hold all evening. The view from the top was quaint, picturesque like that found in a fairytale book, only it was real as we looked down upon the town all lighted, surrounded by the Tatra Mountains and hills. It was like looking into a crystal ball, literally; a fiesta, alive and inspiring in miniature just like in a science-fiction movie, where the camera slowly approaches the edge of the precipice viewing the new arrivals from outer space, we, the somber, secure, enlightened ones. Besides, I forgot to add, the beat of the wild Western music, pouring out from the open windows and doors dashed all poetic thoughts and heightened ridiculous absurdities, quickened our step, to get inside and see just what it was all about. Nearing the lodge, we could feel the ground shake; the mountain was physically vibrating; what I mean to say is that the ground beneath us was rumbling, foreboding; more like trembling, some kind of stimulating enticement, a precursor to a volcanic eruption—our extinction at hand—that we, the young and foolish, couldn't wait to embrace. How weird was that. Yet our pace quickened as we ran up three porch steps.

The building shaking up and down while the people inside were dancing. Through the open windows we saw it all. "Stop! Look, over here, over there; oh, my God, you're right, Maria; you're right," Andrei's voice spiking higher, "it's like a Trampolina."

We all stopped and observed. Everything was moving up and down in timbered rhythm to the rock-'n-roll beat inside. Timbers supporting the quaint, peeked-roofed mountain lodge were creaking enjoyment, like mattress springs, an invite to every deepening bend.

That I never remembered, however, I was much younger and with my parents. They took me here years ago. Well, for sure, there's no generational gap, and now the movement of the Earth beneath us was certainly no illusion. Those old timbered logs were working overtime, keeping time with the music. Laughing we rushed around the porch and into the human jungle gym to get reacquainted with our inner self and other adult children.

Immediately, Pricilla and Donna Rae were dancing with a male counterpart. Why not! Wasn't this what touring was all about: here today, gone tomorrow? Well, maybe not, but that was the feeling, and the atmosphere conveyed much, much more. After the first wild dance, Donna and Pricilla bought drinks for everyone. They each had a margarita; I, a pina colata and a whisky for Andrei. Their two partners declined drinks but had an empty table with their drinks in place; so, we joined them. Beginning to take our dancing and drinking seriously when Andrei leaned over to me and said:

*　　*　　*

"You surprise me."

"How so?"

"I've just heard you play the most fantastic music, and you are here, right now, enjoying this loud, wild American rock music. How can you separate yourself so quickly?"

"Because I'm with you, enjoying the separation of sounds; this is something you are responsible for; this is something you do to me; believe me, never have I felt this relaxed and comfortable before, and I love it. And it's all because of you; you are the first person to have ever made me feel this wild and crazy all at once; I call it comfortable."

"Then can we dance?"

"I'd love to."

The music was a little wild and Maria felt right at home moving and grooving, and, I might say, she was pretty good; of course, why not, she's an accomplished musician and certainly has not a problem moving to the beat. But then the live group on the stage switched to something more accommodating for couple's relaxation and slowed the pace to a rendition of Louis Armstrong's HELLO DOLLY.

And once more, totally unexpected, a little slower still AMOR, VIDA DE MI VIDA. We both were surprised and more so when a tenor began to sing.

"These Polish musicians are quite good."

"They're Spanish musicians, my love; I read in the paper they were on tour, and we happened to book them for the weekend here in Zakopane. Surprised?"

"Definitely! And how appropriate are the words—anticlimactic."

"Perhaps. But let's enjoy the moment."

"Yes, let us. You know, you are a beautiful woman, Maria, and I love you; you know I do; I have been seduced by you forever."

"Now that's a powerful line. I had no idea I had that much influence."

"More than you will ever know, my dear."

And I held her as close as could be, not aware of anyone else on the dance floor.

With the music over, Maria asked if we could go outside, where it's quiet, listen to ourselves talk with no interference.

"Of course," I said. We excused ourselves, and said that we were going to sit outside, maybe on the porch; we'll be nearby. When we started toward the door, Maria interrupted, thinking she had hurt my feelings.

"I thought it was what you wanted to hear, Andrei; we can always go out; sit on the porch, back to the car or just take a walk in the surrounding mountains right here. Truly, I meant no insult to your sensitivities."

"Never an insult, Maria, never from you."

*　　*　　*

As we both stepped out onto the porch, I reached for his hand. Walking toward a big sturdy log corner post that from either direction joined two porch railings, I turned to Andrei.

"I thought you might want to see some of Zakopane just after sunset, to enjoy the outline of the Tatra mountain peaks. They are quite faint but beautiful this time of the evening, poetic in their dramatic stance."

"You're absolutely right; I am enjoying myself, and I thank you; I thank you for everything. I just wanted to sit quietly and talk to you; to get to know you and just how different, far apart we really are from one another. That's all."

"Do you mean how different our lives are?"

"Not only that but our educations, our lifestyles, our goals; I'd like to know for myself how far I must go, so that one day I may meet you on an equal setting. Your music and talent, I can never equal, for you are greatly gifted in a world of your own, and I'm happy for you. Also, no one can get in if you don't want them. I realized that this evening. I'm thrilled I had the chance to hear you play, that I even sat next to you; of course, after you are recognized, no one would ever believe me."

"Andrei, if it were somehow possible, I would have you sit by me every day, before, during, and after rehearsal and . . . ," she abruptly stopped.

"And what?" Andrei quietly asked, standing now one step below her as they continued to talk.

"Share together our lives, our love."

"That I would love, Maria, and I have thought of it."

Continuing to hold hands, we stepped from the porch and slowly, silently, made our way beyond the dim lights of the building, across the open field where the moon was in full light. So bright was it that it made our footing quite easy as we walked toward the shadows of the forest edge. The farther we walked, the quieter it got, until we reached the edge of the big pine grove. Finding a few downed logs, we sat down on one; conveniently we leaned up against another big pine, and admired one another, hiding under massive boughs, just beyond the ring of nature's earthly strobe. We began to talk. Comfortably ensconced with my arm about her, Maria asked:

"What's it like where you live?"

"Actually, Sofija's a big city now, with lots of streets, lights, businesses, people and many tourists, and it's still Communist controlled, you know. They took over after WWII, eliminating many of the aristocracy, many who were very good leaders; good to their mine workers, farm workers, those employed in the businesses about the town and people in general. Bulgaria was slowly growing, slowly beginning to stand up on its own two feet; people were learning new trades, ideas from schools and from the west; that is, from America. Slowly, Bulgaria was rediscovering itself again, giving birth to its once great historic cultural roots, slowly moving toward democracy. But Communism usurped that fledgling freedom; took control, becoming more dominant and crueler; definitely, they were not any less cruel before. After its fall in 1991, communists are still present, but now they are even more sneaky and underhanded; although not as obvious; they disguise everything and now dress themselves as the mafia; smooth, more professional, but, have no doubt, when they ask for something, you give it to them or else. Everything is quite corrupt, and it is hard for a little guy to get started, and if he has a good idea and is successful, they approach him and ask for payment, so he may continue to be able to operate. But if he's just getting by, they let him struggle until he, himself, closes his business.

"And schools are so-so; often teachers will pass a student if he can pay them what he asks. It's not uncommon; everyone knows about it, and so it goes on. In other parts of Europe, a graduate from a Bulgarian high school is not employable; they all know the set up. The goal of the school system in Bulgaria is to make us all equal, all the same; even with a Ph.D., your pay is minimal. I know one who teaches science and is paid 300.00 a month. For example: If I were to leave Sofia and just go job hunting, I would best qualify washing dishes in some French restaurant."

"Andrei, that's incredible; your life is a jail cell; you're all egalitarians—all commonly equal—talent or not, brains or not. You're treated like cattle. Your life has no exit. Oh, I feel sorry for you and your family, your mother and father, your brothers and sisters."

"My one brother is now working in England; my father, a teacher of history, died last year; that is, he left us and returned to Russia. My mother and one sister are still at home. She is mentally challenged, deprived of oxygen at birth and is slow; mentally only about seven years old, although physically older."

That was all I could tell her; my God that was more than enough, but she might as well know, yet I did not want to make myself look foolish in her eyes, seeking sympathy, especially after such a vibrant and memorable concert she gave for me. After all, let's be honest, I'm in love with Maria, and it so happens that she is blessed by the gods with marvelous talent. Euterpe and Apollo, her teachers, are surely proud of her. So sincere than most other girls that I've met. And I cannot believe that she has time for me.

Astonished, I didn't know what to say to him for fear of looking ridiculous, not knowing to what depth that such "isms" still prevail throughout much of the known world today.

"Truly, Andrei, I have been sheltered, leading a wonderful life in America. Yet, I know the suffering the Polish people have endured from what my mother has always told me; unbelievable stories I have heard when visiting with my Aunty Marsha. Throughout history, special men step forward, lock down their pride and secret envy, to do the right thing.

"There was a time when King Stanislaw Sobieski's was asked and consented to help his neighbors to the west. Against all obstacles, he arrived in Vienna just in time, as Commander-in-Chief, confronting the center of the

Turkish Muslin forces, with the Prussian and Austrian army one on either flank, helped saved Vienna in 1683 A.D. To this day, no one in Vienna has ever recognized his great accomplishment and that of his army in terms of any statue of visual commemoration—but my mother has said something is in the works; a plaque and a statue of Sobieski himself. Something has to be done to recognize such determination and sacrifice for freedom, albeit three hundred years later. And how true is it better later than never."

Andrei smiled approval.

"Sometimes when Mother would tell the story, I would flinch to think that perhaps Mozart, himself, may never have had the opportunity to flourish a hundred years later, and, oh, how dreadful for music, for the world."

"You are fortunate to have a mother so interested in keeping and acknowledging her heritage to pass its richness on to you. This is very important, and another reason you play Chopin with such understanding and depth."

"Mother loved to tell that historic story, stressing ideally that people of all nations can all work together, and she was quite good in relating details. Making known, under Kosciusko's military leadership that Poland wanted to improve the lot of the serfs and give them more democratic say, freedom to own land, but Catherine of Russia also afraid that if this idea took hold, it might spread to an uprising of Russian serfs. Poland had to be conquered, quartered and crushed.

"A hundred years after Sobieski's supreme feat in helping his Viennese neighbors, he was turned upon. Austria, Prussia and the Russians secretly agreed to unleash their armies to conquer and divide Poland amongst themselves, hence, no more Poland. Insanity took place with more war and cruelty. 'People,' Mother always told me, 'were put upon Earth to learn to be good to themselves and one another; to help to share; to do good, that is real happiness.' She was always so proud of her heritage, her homeland, as are you. I must have heard these stories, Andrei, a hundred times if not once, but never did I get bored. Those stories about Kosciusko and Pulaski's role in the American Revolution urged me to read more and learn more about my homeland. It was Kosciusko who left his father's farm and went to help Washington fight the British; when he returned to Poland, he instigated a lot of havoc in behalf of Polish freedom against the Russian occupying armies. Against too many too well-armed forces, his little band, determined as they were, was unsuccessful.

"The Polish love of freedom was truly tied to America, and, at that time, America was the underdog, yet they won their independence. Because they were great allies, in the years to come after WWII, the Americans provided open doors, Green Cards and opportunities, for the Poles to come to America to work; to return home or become citizens; either way they made money, saved money. Many returned home, with thirty-five to forty thousand dollars, sometimes more, sewn inside the lining of their heavy overcoats. During the nineteen-fifties, sixties, and seventies, it was not uncommon to give the Russian immigration official a Benjamin; then enter the country with no hassle, often with a new Volkswagen. These returnees became wealthy men, for a one-hundred dred American dollar bill was worth one thousand Polish Zloty. The money was put into the land and their farms; slowly over many years they began to prosper. Today we see the fruit of their struggles.

"Andrei, I am a very spoiled, a lucky girl, to be born and raised in America."

"There's no disgrace in that; that is as it is."

"If there were only some way I could help you."

"That I and my family could get to America would be wonderful. But the time for that happening is not yet."

"You know, Andrei, I'm big on one's heritage; I believe it's the best and most inspiring cornerstone of one's life, at least that's what my grandfather, Sven, says. Whenever he gets on his 'high horse,' Grandfather begins telling us that he's one of the descendants of Quetzalcoatl, leader of the great Caucasian race. This brilliant group of early settlers from another solar system, or, perhaps, from somewhere deep within ours, or a nearby star, eons ago, initially settled in the South Sea Islands, Paradise, along with many other clans of color and culture. When volcanic eruptions started to tease the area, Quetzalcoatl and his followers left Paradise and made an effort to settle in Columbia, but the pigmies were too fearsome; so the unwelcome made a temporary peace; within the next four to six months they built their ships and sailed down the Amazon sea and were gone, settling far away to Norway, Sweden, Finland."

"Maria, wait; you lost me at Amazon Sea; I thought it was the Amazon River."

"Yes, now it's a river; but I'm talking earlier when it was a sea flowing from the Pacific to the Atlantic Ocean."

"And when was this?"

"At least 70,000 to 50,000 thousand years ago."

"B.C.?"

"Of course; it was before the Rockies were established, before the gas belts in the Caribbean blew out with such furry that the West Coast Mountains erupted, about 12,000 B.C.; the eruption was so powerful that it sunk the three massive islands in the Pacific, which together composed a land mass larger than North America and Mexico; some 64,000,000 died."

"What have you been reading, my dear Maria?"

"Oh, Mother used to tease Grandpa Sven, her father-in law, asking, 'Why so far North? It must have been the fishing, right?' In good humor my grandpa answered, 'Yes, of course, that too.' Then he'd go on telling how they, Quetzalcoatl and the Caucasian race, escaped to Latvia, eventually populating into Russia; then to Germany, France and Poland and as far down as Greece. Definitely, they continued west into Ireland, Scotland, and England. Supposedly there were 12 tribes, initially; then there is talk of 72, but each went his separate way. Some made their way from the three islands in the Pacific, West via China, some to Africa, India, the Middle East, the Mediterranean and western and southern Europe. The world's physical landscape was totally unsettled from the many volcanic upheavals.

"Many American natives came straight over from the islands; some through the Bering Strait. For us our giveaway trademark was our white skin, blue or green eyes, blonde or red hair and, for a few exceptions, freckles. Interesting, though, most of the Chinese students I met while in college all stressed the importance of protecting their white skin, emphasizing that the original rulers were white skinned; so they always wore big hats, long sleeves and pants to protect their skin, avoiding the sun by all means. Silly it is, but that was what I saw and heard in conversation."

"That's a lot to take in; very interesting, but what do you mean by 'high horse'?"

"That's when my grandfather would talk about his heritage, telling us what a wonderful line of intelligent people he came from: peaceful, non-warlike. Being the Swede that he was, he always emphasized his physical characteristics; and my mother, also, as physical proof; though I must admit both were quite intelligent; my mother naturally was a wonderful pianist, and Sven, my grandfather on my father's side, was a mathematician. So, there you have it. More importantly, what about you; I'm sure you have more to say. Somewhere in your heritage eons ago, you, too, were part of this great movement from the Pacific Paradise. So, tell me."

"If I recall correctly, I believe Donna Rae told me that you were a double major, true?"

"Music and Biology."

"That's marvelous! But why two majors?"

"Just in case my piano career doesn't materialize, I have something practical to fall back on. It was, also, the suggestion of both my mother and father, Grandfather also concurred."

*　　*　　*

"Okay, you clever one, now that you've tricked me into jabbering about my background, it's your turn. No more coaxing from me; I find you totally capable of talking for yourself; I want to know more, much more about your heritage, come on now, out with it. There's no disgrace that you were born in Bulgaria; that's the way it is. Tell me right from the beginning about your family and their background, their history; so, talk, Mr. Andrei Ivanov, much as you can remember. The night is young; and now that we are together, I'm determined to know more about you."

*　　*　　*

For sure she's direct, says what she thinks; I like that, and, yet, she's soft and encouraging, never overbearing. I want to know her, truly; however, she's right. Quite flimsy of me to quiet down and back away; that certainly doesn't work with this lady. Maria truly knows that the quickest way to cross the street is a straight path; if one doesn't exist, she'll make one; if someone needs help, she's there. There's a lot of home in her—she would be a great partner for life.

"Well, I was born in the little town of Pernik, east of Sofia."

"Actually, Pernik, Bulgaria, was at the far western end of my mother's great-grandfather's farm. His name was Ilia Zafirov, and his farm stretched from Pernik all the way to the western outskirts of Sofija, about forty-two kilometers."

37

"Wow! That's quite a spread as the cowboys out west would say; that's about twenty-six miles."

"Yes, you're right, about twenty-six miles and a little more than half as wide, about eighteen miles. It was a very large piece of property."

Maria sat quietly as Andrei continued to expand on his background; she was pleasantly surprised when he began back in the 1860s with his great-great grandfather, Ilia. All the while he spoke, Maria could see his pride walk forth, rising excitedly like that of a happy child talking about his favorite things; and she loved the enthusiastic animation of his energetic mind. Instantly, she knew he had marvelous potential. So proud of his mother's grandfather, as I am sure he's heard many firsthand tales from her.

"King Boris the III was more than pleased with Ilia's expanded productions and yields to feed his country's development and new progress. And Ilia had increased employment to eight hundred people. Progress was real."

"So, you have an aristocratic background; I'm happy for you."

"But it was not always that way, Maria. Let me continue, so you can draw your own conclusions."

"Before all this success took place, Ilia worked on this great estate since he was a little boy, learning all aspect of the great farm and its management while working with his father. Having worked all areas of the land, he became invaluable and respected by his aristocratic employer. When the Russian-Turkish war ended, unfavorably for Turkey, in 1878, Bulgaria, once more, had its freedom; but it was a disastrous situation for the Turks; obvious, the Turkish army and the grand Turkish aristocracy had to abandon Bulgaria, nothing but their personal things could they take, and the Turkish owner gave his entire estate, everything, to Ilia. The number-one reason being the loss of the war, but also Ilia was a loyal employee, very honest. His employer always trusted him and was dependent on his good judgment. So, there may have been some consolation, that, at least, the great farm was passed into good hands, to a good an honorable trustee of the land."

While listening, Maria innocently snuggled herself closer to Andrei. She didn't even think of what he may have thought; she just did it, and, to her surprise, she fit perfectly with her head up against his shoulder, so restful that she could hear his heartbeats begin to quicken.

"Are you comfortable?" he affectionately asked, as he moved to wrap his right arm about her, snuggling her closer, making them both cozy. "Now isn't that better?"

"Much better, thank you," she smiled.

From a musical point of view, Maria loved the sound of Andrei's melodic baritone voice, so soothing and sincere. In a remote corner of her womanly mind, never so bold was she, but to her way of thinking, now, it was all so natural. With eyes wide open, she listened.

"Nowadays the business of farming was not just for the military, but for the people too, for their new progress of business, manufacturing, and rebuilding their ancient country anew. A magnificent farming estate that was in the high spirit of production contributing to its nation; there was nothing like it, possibly, throughout the entire country. It was a golden place that was divided into seven large districts: sheep and cows, hogs; butchering, sausage making; dairy products with cheeses and whey; wheat production; barley, grains, and vegetables: potatoes, beans. It was an industrial food supply for sale in the city; Great-Great-Grandpa Ilia employed eight hundred people. Of course, King Boris III was extremely proud of this great success. Ilia's son, Krum, continued to grow the estate, and Boris the III and Krum became good friends. When the King could not be found signing documents running the country, good chance was, he was over to Krum's plantation. With no telephones, the Royal one just dropped by, and two fast friends became lost. Riding over the land together was not unusual for them, discussing production or what was being planned for the fall harvest festival or the upcoming Christmas, New Year's gatherings, looking farther into the spring, it was Easter, and its glorious rebirth. Sometimes Boris III just stopped by for a bowl of soup and a good piece of homemade bread, followed with a good cup of coffee and the traditional favorite: fresh-baked Bulgarian Banitsa served hot. At the house, Boris had proven himself repeatedly a man of the soil."

"I remember my father saying, 'People have to eat, that's essential,'" Maria interjected.

"No truer fact. My mother's mother told her that the grapes were always exceptional, and, depending on the yield, good wine was either sold or saved for the great harvest festival and holiday gatherings, each year adding to or replenishing the last successful harvest.

"It was a four-season climate, on latitude of northern Nebraska, I believe, and agriculture was a burgeoning business; as organized as this plantation was, it did not do away with many of the little farmers because Bulgaria was an agrarian country.

"Krum also became an importer of Singer sewing machines, acquiring the franchise for all of Southeastern Europe in 1908, only fifty-seven years since it was first invented. On the other hand, engaging enterprise is what a free country does; it expresses Great Spirit and pride in one's country as to one that is not free. Hand sewing, stitching, painstakingly close work was monotonous, painful at times. But all that drudgery was being replaced with a Singer; it revolutionized the manufacturing of clothing, literally. Those sweat shops were updated shops; in other words, productivity increased and prices did come down a little, with labor being cut, more was being done by less, but the big production shops were to be the product of another story that's familiar with the United States industries. Truly, America is blessed."

"We are. It's still the land of opportunity."

"If you are not afraid to work and do, I've heard you can be successful."

"Andrei, you must come to America."

"Believe me, I do want to."

"I do believe you."

"Nice as the thought is, I have obligations."

"But you will solve them. I will help, Andrei. And the time is near when I will be able to."

"No, this is my problem, not yours. Thank you for the offer."

"A very proud aristocrat you are," she managed with a gently folded fist of her left hand to give him a few tender love taps in circular motion over his heart for encouragement, expressing her pride in him as he lovingly squeezed her a little closer and kissed the top of her forehead.

"Way back when, during another time maybe, and now, no more; thanks to the cruel Germans and then the demonic and incompetent Communists, all is gone."

"But still, you are an aristocrat."

"No, I am not," he softly pleaded, slightly shaking his head, trying to make this darling one understand. What he didn't grasp was that she understood very well; what he did understand was that Maria possessed a certain sweetness that is its own reward, if one is brave.

"Okay. Way back when, before your time, your family inherited an estate; they didn't illegally invade another land, plundering the countryside or kill anyone, it was bequeathed to your family because it was probably originally yours to begin with; and once back in Ilia's hands, your great-grandfather increased its productivity; his son, Krum, continued to develop the estate, and also hobnobbed with King Boris III, participating in his society, rubbing shoulders with his family and friends. Krum became very wealthy; he owned a great estate that the King, himself, enjoyed to ride over and took great pleasure in its wise development. All this is wealth, and this type of wealth always finds ways to continue to grow, to expand. This is what surrounds aristocracy, Andrei. And Boris and Krum palled around over the golden estate of your Great-Great Grandfather Ilia Zafirov's. And his son, Krum, earned big money and was good to his employees: he's an aristocrat and by heritage so are you and your family. Oh, my," Maria sat up as if suddenly aware of her nonchalant manner. "I better watch my manners; I'm in the company of an aristocrat, no less royalty, if you dig deep enough; it's bred in the people of your ancestral heritage," smiling at the handsome one, her bright eyes luminous, a renaissance firing the imagination of his heritage, exciting the dancer from Bulgaria, thoughts that he never would have dared to encounter except for the spirited, beautiful woman sitting next to him that he found hard to believe loved him, at least that was his take.

"Now you're playing with me."

"Not at all; it is not uncommon for great families to lose their positions, become subservient under harsher conditions, then fate somehow restores them to their rightful place, or they choose another path and become very successful again. Not an impossible happening, Andrei."

"You make me feel like there's hope."

"There is always hope when human beings act like human beings."

"You're a philosopher too."

"As my grandfather would say, 'Of course, I'm part of the great early forerunners of the Caucasian race.'"

"I like your grandfather already, and I have never met him."

How pleasant was the quiet with each thinking pleasant thoughts of the other, feeling the warmth and nearness of each, while willingly exposing self as sincere lovers do, so, she continued.

"My curiosity wants to know why the earring in your left ear, an endearing remembrance? Tell me its story."

"In the Russian military, one is not permitted to wear such jewelry, nothing at all. When I was drafted into the army, I wore it against the rules. Actually, it was deliberately worn in an act of defiance, for I despised everything Russian and Communist. I was caught, told to take it out. When I refused, they beat me up. So now I wear it as a deliberate sign of my hate for their corrupt, destructive occupation of Bulgaria. However, when I now think about it, it's like a tattoo, except this one I can remove to be presentable while the poor idiots who mark themselves crazy, can never completely remove all their silly bodily marks or lover's imprints.

"What if they break up or wake up, find a new love; how do they explain away old love markings? Sometimes, I'll ask one just what does this or that tattoo mean. Usually, they tell me it's a reminder of some past love, a dear one, a close friend. I say nothing but think to myself, they have no brain, at least no memory recall; probably because they blew away whatever little they had with drugs. What an idiot, that's something the natives do in the jungles of New Guinea, justifiably, being creative for real boredom."

They moved away from their log seats to a more comfortable bench overlooking Zakopane. Sublimely, each wondered how to convey deeper feeling to a better, a more fulfilling conclusion; one afraid of being too pushy; the other afraid of being too easy. So, they fell back on their growing honesty and comfort. From the goodness of each trust grew, and so did their love, each wanting to be part of the other's goodness.

Andrei has all the ingredients, Maria believed, to be a self-made success; he just needs a little encouragement, a push, conversational guidance and love, sincere and real.

Skipping, running in circular fashion, like lost, intoxicated, shadowy specters, floating, drifting while looking for someone, Donna Rae and Pricilla joined us; too exhilarated, they asked, "So what do we do next?"

"How about an all-nighter," queried Pricilla.

"Too demanding," countered Donna Rae, "besides we have a plane to catch tomorrow; why not go back to the house and just listen to music and Aunty Marsha wakes us at six; it's only three and a half hours away; maybe this time I'll sleep soundly on the return flight to London."

"Not a bad idea," sung slightly intoxicated Pricilla.

"The all-nighter or catching a little shut eye," accorded Donna Rae, looking at Maria and Andrei.

"Have either of you seen the moon?" asked Maria.

"What moon?" both asked.

"Oh, that moon," Pricilla nudged Donna Rae, who after a moment or two got the idea she was supposed to respond, "Oh, gee, that moon," as they both giggled themselves silly.

"Seeing that I'm the designated driver, I suggest heading back to the house and continue talking, eating or sleeping."

Chapter Five

Auf Wiedersehen

An easy decision it was, an honest admittance that all young bodies sometimes tire. Andrei thought of a play within a play in which he was now participating. Soon the final curtain will fall, and the players will leave. Three lovely ladies exit the stage in Zakopane; home they go to perform in another play where lives are meaningful and exciting; especially Maria who is on to a fabulous concert career that one day, perhaps, he will sit and enjoy as part of the audience; that is, when she is performing in Vienna. What a wonderful thought that he will have known this accomplished lady who once held his hand and shared a kiss.

No one will believe him, if he should tell them, but this is a dream forever his that he will always keep.

Aunty Marsha asked if anyone was hungry; of course, they all said yes. When all was confirmed, Aunty knew exactly what to do; it was potato pancakes with eggs and Uncle Walter's homemade double-smoked bacon and his Polish Kielbasa. It was four A.M.; everyone ate as if it were his last meal.

"Did you see Andrei's troupe perform?" Donna Rae blurted to Aunty Marsha.

"You bet I did. Yetta called and told me not to miss it; 'Father Wronka,' she said, 'wanted everyone to see the beautiful performers from Sofiya.' No one was disappointed. Quite surprised and very impressed, especially with the

Mazowsze performance of MUZYCZKA (MUSIC) and CYRANECZKA (THE LITTLE WILD DUCK). And Mr. Andrei, here, was wonderful, just wonderful. I have an idea, Andrei, why don't you stay in Poland and perform with our folklore troupe next year; teach us some of your dances, and we will teach you ours; that way Maria and her friends will have to return. Good idea? Yes, no?"

"I would like that very much," smiled Andrei.

"Anything is possible," added Pricilla.

"It would be nice," Maria touched Andrei's hand and planted an unpretentious kiss on his unsuspecting right cheek; a simple, precious act of love; he glowed, confirming what everyone already knew: that they were in love.

Thanks to Aunty Marsha, the girl's clothing was already washed and pressed, neatly laid out ready to be packed. Thank-you from everyone, even I was a bit envious—washed and pressed clean clothing. But, then, we had facilities; although, sometimes, we had to find one, and then do our own laundry; however, one was usually to be had at our place of stay.

So, I remained on the sofa in the living room waiting for Maria to return; it wasn't long as she had just one suitcase.

"One suitcase! Oh, my, you are a traveler par excellence, a pro. I like that. Pack a case and travel."

Smiling, Maria was pleased with my compliment then confessed that she had her own closet here. "Why not, it's my aunt's house, and she, too, has things at our house in Chicago."

Maria sat down beside me. Grasping hands, I kissed long graceful fingers; they were warm and her heart warmer.

When you want it to be forever or just a wee bit longer, time always moves too quickly, ask anyone in love. A little longer to tell another story; a little longer to hear another answer or to just be together for another minute; to love and linger in the emotion, knowing it's the right thing to do; then leaving, devastating. Oh, would it were night again as we look into love's eyes, seeking some excuse to stop time, chiding inwardly for not taking advantage of what is now our discovery; if only to run to another room to love, as we know we are passionately ready. But time restricts our love; it waits for no one; so, we had our chance, so there. To lovers they act disappointed or, in-discriminately, often in haste, because they know that they are time itself running out.

Theoretically, there is another option, though; a chancy one: that is for another time because time is infinite, forever, permanent, constant, undeniable present; for it is we who act in time, move through time, change and are saved in time; therefore, we will have another opportunity if we choose. But, in order to do so, we must make a plan and take the risk.

In Maria, Andrei sees a spirit, a beauty that naturally emanates deep from within. Her consummate, illuminating performance of Chopin that ties their two souls to a sensitivity that brings forward what man insists on keeping dim. Her particular sense of pleasure is not only sensual, but her intellectual guise reveals adventure to live her life to its full capacity. A true and powerful humanist as is the nature of every contributing woman, the more gifted the more that makes her what she is, beautiful. That Maria knows exactly where she is going; an example he must bend to himself and keep focused.

*　　*　　*

On the way to the Krakow airport, Maria asked if there are certain things that cannot be brought into Bulgaria.

"I'm sure there are restrictions."

"Indeed, there are, but one has just to pay the border guard; he then pays his boss, and in comes anything, most particular is the newest computer equipment, televisions, tape recorders, record players and the music to play on them."

"But you said that, individually, your troupe earns almost nothing while on tour; it's all paid for by the State."

"That's true, but we earn money elsewhere."

"What do you mean?"

"We perform in certain town squares in the evening; sometimes during the afternoon when we're not performing. And the tourists are wonderful to us."

"That's quite creative and very American."

"True, though unlike America, if we get caught, we can go to jail, all monies confiscated. You'd be surprised."

"Not really. Are the crowds good?"

"Oh, yes, yes, they are, and the people are very generous; not impossible

47

for us to make five hundred dollars a performance."

"Exciting, but if you get caught."

"We lose all; or just give up a little and no jail."

"It's fun putting yourselves out there but chancy, and not the preferred way you want to earn a living, I imagine."

"Not at all, but it helps us buy the things we want."

"Little progress in the country, I assume."

"Absolutely, although my mother says since the time, she was a little girl, and even earlier, things are still the same; there has been no progress in the past eighty years or more. When you look about, it's all the same. Vulgar construction of dull grey cement block buildings next to glorious, ancient structures of a thousand years and some much, much older. They want to demolish all, to make way for utilitarian structures for the new egalitarian society of Communism. They are unlearned, uneducated, ignorant fools led by uneducated, narrow-minded, ignorant political imbeciles. They want no one to enjoy let alone to trace his heritage to its glorious past. If you do away with one's heritage, you do away with civilized society. Heritage is a great sounding board, a cornerstone of one's origins, one's family, community, religion; moral and ethical education; without these there is no educational opportunity: in short, no human growth, only simple animals acquiescing."

"Oh, I wish I could take you and your family to America; yet I have no idea how difficult it is for all of you, especially you who have such talent and great promise. We will keep contact."

They embrace the natural request of their souls seen through their eyes; they hold each other tight, releasing their embrace a little to look into each other's eyes, and then answer the inevitable call to kiss.

"I kiss'd you once restful calamity."

"On the bench before the piano, Andrei, as I recall it was such sweet warmth, unmatched singularity."

"And we'll continue these lines the next time we meet."

Once more, pausing to embrace and kiss passion's request, trying to seal out the long-coming absence as neither wanted to admit but knew too well.

"I'm looking forward to it. I love you, Andrei."

"As do I love you, my love."

"Auf Wiedersehen."

"Forget me not, Maria."

"Never, Andrei, never!"

They embraced, each wishing for more time, each promising to keep contact.

Sweet, yes, each wanting the other, but not enough sweetness; division so great, one cannot believe how great. For one returns to nothing; the other returns to everything and every opportunity to achieve. Indeed, a somber situation it was; in waiting, too much time lost between two different worlds.

"You are beautiful, talented and truly a wonderful person, Maria; your soul is beautiful, complete; no matter where you go, or whatever you do, your soul will remain virginal to your love's reflection. I cannot believe what I have witnessed here this past evening with you; that you have let me participate. I feel honored, believe me. You are a wonderful pianist, and I look forward to seeing you play on the professional stage because, regardless of what your instructor says, you're ready now. May I write to you; do you think that you'll have time in your full schedule? If you don't, I will definitely understand. I love you, but, remember, we're in two different worlds on two different continents, but things can work out. If it doesn't, thank you; thank you so very much, Maria. You will always be in my prayers. Yet, I have this feeling that we'll meet again, but you know all lovers say that; and that's probably true, for we romantics are a hopeless lot."

"Yes, we are, and, yes, I will keep contact. I love you, Andrei Ivanov. Until we meet again, and like you, I know we will."

For the last time they kissed long and passionate, hungrily holding one another long and tight both tearing; anyone who saw them, doubtless, knew they were not just hello and goodbye lovers with false rapture; they were lovers truly in love as two worlds collide knowing not how to disengage, so they fragment.

Chapter Six

Together Once More

Her piano playing was astounding for one so young. From the very beginning with her mother's careful schooling, Maria caught on easily and quickly, more than a penchant of natural talent, which Mother had noted from the very beginning, and so she slowly nurtured her talented daughter as best she could, by showing and encouraging Maria's beautiful hands, that naturally ranged over the keyboard better than an octave, proper fingering technique to keep their control and accuracy and gracefulness when engaging complicated passages. And never would one suspect such physical dynamics, such sound from her black ivory-studded cat responding her expression, her poetic will. Varieties of shading too numerous to mention let alone comprehend, yet generating magic, captivating the listener to the depths of his soul where lust and true love blend as one.

Another year and another dazzling European summer; and once more Maria was scheduled to play two concerts in Vienna in the very same place where last year, she made her première at the beautiful Auersperg Palais. Of course, she sent Andrei tickets to attend her première, and in the letter expressed disappointment that management would not permit him to sit next to her. Afterwards he was at the reception honoring her great success. Although they could not be alone for the demands of her success—its confusion of her newfound admirers; however, they did manage to shake hands, briefly converse and embrace while at the same time he kissed her cheek, then quickly they embraced a passionate kiss. When he turned to leave, she put her new home address in New York into his hand. Their hearts were breaking, but he had to leave to return to Zurich for tomorrow's performance, but next year at the same time the Bulgarian Troupe was also scheduled to perform in Vienna, but somewhere outside also within the first circle of the Old Town Square. Through their correspondence, it was confirmed as to schedules-influence strongly by each: she upon her insistence to her manager and he to his troupe director. And so, a little miracle was to happen.

Always checking the billboards wherever his troupe performed, Andrei was excited to find that Maria was scheduled again to play two concerts at the Auersperg Palais; and, yes, he did pay to hear and see her perform that evening, marveling at her talent. It was a beautiful concert, sold out and the crowd appreciative; applause was full and gratifying, encouraging to her and her managing entourage; the performance was a great success.

Afterwards there was no chance to see Maria personally; rather the appreciative crowd completely surrounded her exit, hanging about the stage door for a glimpse of the talented one who is so breathtakingly beautiful. But escort had her well in hand, letting no one get near her save for a few handshakes and autographs. Andrei waved to her, but she never saw him; then he returned to his troupe.

The following day, Maria had found a way, via the stage manager, to get a ticket to Andrei for her performance that afternoon. As she exited the stage door, she saw Andrei. Going ahead of her manager and her mother, her chaperone, Maria, moved toward him and professionally signed his program: "See you tonight, Love Maria." Then she was whisked away into a waiting automobile.

Once more, Andrei returned to his troupe, for this evening they were performing songs and dances of Bulgaria.

Earlier, Maria saw his performance poster and their performance time; she had seen a flyer and heard a few offhand comments; inquiring confirmation of her stage manager, after her afternoon concert, she asked what was going on this evening in the old town square, for she saw outside seating being arranged.

"It's a Bulgarian Troupe, my lady; and they're quite good."

"Really?"

"Seeing that you love music, you would enjoy them; I've seen them before; they are quite spontaneous; performance begins at nine P.M. You have no performance this evening so that will be convenient."

And there you have it. Call it whatever you want, but, for certain, it was not coincidental; yet each still thinking of the other, earlier, remotely, now for certain during the festive excitement of a Viennese summer evening.

Maria was full with excitement at once more seeing Andrei dance; his strong graceful flow of masculine movement. But this time she knew that they wanted more time together. Thinking if only if yesterday were today and last year now and it would be tonight once more, but it wasn't because reality had set in; after all, it was two years later, actually, beginning now the third year.

A light punch was served afterwards, and the appreciative crowd, amazed at the vigor of the performers, enjoyed themselves in good international spirit gregariously emptied the punch bowls. Amid comments of "congratulations, marvelous dancing," as if right on cue, Maria and Andrei met one another walking out of the crowd toward the same punch table.

Instantly, all their wishes were granted. Heaven smiled. Each reached for the other's hand; quickly the two slipped away from the crowded square and down a little side street out of sight where they longingly, passionately embraced, smothering long-overdue conversations with ardent kisses, crossing over all that echoed before and now flowed under. Each began to tear, embracing frantic, not believing their good luck, the end game from which all good actions now will emerge.

"It's been too long, Maria."

"Yet the gap is closed, even if it's only for a moment. I'm married, Andrei."

"I too and I have a child, a girl, but I don't think she has any of your talent."

An emotional laugh as if that had anything to do with their lives.

"As long as she's healthy and has your guidance, she will be successful, my love."

"Thank you, I needed that. But are you happy, my dear?"

"I am, I believe," hesitant, the beautiful pianist, averted her heavenly blue eyes answering quietly, slowly, "yes, I believe, I think I am." Turning the question away, Maria asked: "And you are you happy, Andrei?"

"For the moments I'm with you now, very happy once more."

"I meant your . . . ."

"Marriage? It's okay for now."

"I'm prying. Andrei, I'm sorry; forget what was said, it's past. It's all about us here and now, this moment."

"I saw your performance yesterday afternoon; you are marvelous."

"Thank you. How did you know where we were performing tonight?"

"I wanted to be sure so I asked and the stage manager about the seating I saw in the square; he told me that the Bulgarian Troupe was performing again tonight, and I wanted to see and be with you once more. It was some time before I exited the stage door yesterday evening, and when I did, I looked over the crowd, and I thought I saw you going away. Instinctive feelings returned to me just like our first time. I began to feel excited, tingly, a stirring of my emotions all like before when we were first together."

"I feel like I'm a spinning top, Maria, standing on my head looking at you, holding you, all a dither, awhirl. You're here alone?"

"Yes, finally. You know my husband's my coach and agent."

"I know; you mentioned it in your letter."

"He had a planning meeting to attend. How convenient, I thought; it's Providence. Yet, I know that you never believe in coincidence, a fluke."

"I do not. But Providence is tied to the Creator, mover of the universe, and much more powerful than just a casual meeting or chance occurrence."

"Agreed!" Smiling, they embraced again; he continued whispering to her.

"Your performance this afternoon was brilliant; just as it was yesterday evening. There was quite a crowd this afternoon, too."

"As there is tonight for your troupe," looking at him. "And how much better my playing if you were sitting next to me. Oh, Andrei, I've missed you terribly, terribly."

"And I you," still tearing.

Hugging tightly once more, slowly continuing down a quiet, charming alleyway where we found a tiny coffee shop. Sitting quietly side-by-side in the little booth, each holding the other's arm, the other's hand, our heads tilted to touching. Two lovers again kissing, truly loving lips while soul's yearning bless body's request. Each with his Viennese coffee shared the other's delicious apple strudel silently talking. Excited once more with our union, affirming our bond never had been broken; confessing how we might do it all over again; making changes that were too formidable at the time. Compliant eyes longing, urging to fulfill reflecting spirit's natural demand.

"Tomorrow, Andrei, I leave for Prague, Paris, and Zurich."

"I for Munich, Budapest, Zagreb."

With burning resolve never again to lose contact. Maria promised Andrei that whenever she performed an encore, the very last piece would always be Chopin's PRELUDE IN A MAJOR.

"I know the one, Opus 28; it's very short but very deep, full of love."

"Yes, it is ours forever to recall the consummation of our love."

As embers fire lovers' hearts, Maria remembered two years before the way Andrei looked at her, the same way she looked at him that evening in the rehearsal hall when sitting together on the piano bench; when their hearts opened to one another; when their love expressed openly with his first kiss that she willingly returned; that same way he looked at her now. Without hesitation, they closed the door and loved the night.

Chapter Seven

Separate Ways

Of course, Miles Davis and company and good whisky, always made good jazz better. It was the proper sound and the proper place for upcoming artists to present, not only their jazz but their painting, sculpture, photography. The little hole in the wall was just around the corner of the main downtown tourist walks, with good local walk-in traffic; and more walk-in traffic from the industrial business district down the block, my business was good and slowly growing.

I got into the bar business a couple of years after the fall of the Berlin Wall in 1989; the communist government resigned and free elections were promised in the spring; everything was wild, wide open. So, to supply my bar with booze I became a bootlegger. Now there was a life that was truly more exciting than it was ever meant to be, particularly when I was running and sneaking liquor into Bulgaria illegally. Driving over snowy, slippery iced roads just to make a buck; and there was one time a big blizzard, just before Christmas, nearly a whiteout. Seeing that I could make out the front of my two-seat Dolphin, I stupidly concluded why not, I can make it; it's not really a whiteout, I remember saying to myself when I began to skid to one side. Bumping off the mountain the car and I, as if by magic, for I had no control, continued slowly sliding, going so slow or maybe so terrible fast that I saw my entire life up to that moment passing before me. Honestly, I have no idea how the car did not go off the edge and into the ravine, three hundred feet below. Bottom line, I was lucky and the money was good, really good. Also, I was young and eager to make a success of my life. Every month I was delivering to over a hundred stores, bootleg operations and night time jazz clubs. The crooked income kept the family afloat, but my wife didn't like that I was sharing and supporting my mother and sister too.

So, to make things simple, she divorced me; then the girlfriend returned to England and her parents, taking with her our only daughter. Little did I know it would be over twenty years before I saw her again.

After the divorce, Mother and I went to lunch; it was here that she told me not to carry a grudge; not to hate because that alone will kill you; so, it was not meant to be. It was good advice, and she was right. On the other hand, my bar contacts were good; everything was beginning to pay off. I paid my dues, you might say. So far, the mafia contacts were also good; I was now part of the gang. My little one-room bar business continued vibrating.

I felt so good that I began to occasionally smoke a cigar, but that was during the wee hours of the morning when sitting with my friends, talking softly, planning and listening to great jazz. Although I was trying, it was taking a little time to attract some live music: a little jazz trio or quartet in particular. I was open to all suggestions and not opposed to listening to all kinds of good music. When the musicians went home, close friends and I sat around and listened to jazz CDs. Yes, we even got attached to certain operas and loved to hear the greats such as Victoria de Los Angeles and Jussi Bjoerling and their incomprehensible MADAMA BUTTERFLY or LA Bohéme. We were all dazzled to have such classics; immediately we praised the genius of modern technology and wanted to make a comparison of these two voices to other operatic singers who sang the same opera. It was a normal intellectual bent for those who love to be in the know of who or which was better. It was all good, but one time I was definitely stirred when my lady friend, Grace, brought in a Lynne Arriale Trio CD, titled: WHEN YOU LISTEN, which she had gotten through the Black Market—where we got all of our CDs.

*   *   *

Seeing that Grace purchased it, it was hers, and she was in charge of choosing her favorite selections; instead of jumping around, she began from the beginning because "I would love it," she said.

"Really?" I asked.

"Really, it's the kind of music that makes you just want to curl up or sit alone in corner and reminisce, thinking of the one that got away and what went wrong."

On it went. Instantly, I was confused, frowning. For I heard someone, somewhere, a long time ago, mention that she enjoyed the playing of the Lynne Arriale Trio, especially Lynne on the piano. "Not only was she graceful, delicate and strong, but her interpretation of BESS YOU IS MY WOMAN NOW was magical, personal to everyone once or forever now in love." Then I remembered the voice was Maria's.

It was she who told me of the Lynne Arriale Trio. When first I heard it played, as I have never heard it before, I just stopped whatever I was thinking; one of my friends slipped me a whisky, and I saw Maria sitting to my left. Red hair, crimson cheeks slightly freckled, magnificent deep blue eyes, oh, she was beautiful, radiant, and I was lost. Strength and determination, I could hear in the next cut: YOU AND THE NIGHT AND THE MUSIC. Leaning back, I listened to Maria playing. About the table everyone quiet, enjoying, but I was there by her side, again. I'm sure to a musician sensitive as was Maria, she could interpret feelings more meaningful than just the way chords and notes were written; and when she played truly, she painted a world all its own. I began to wonder when listening to LONELY WOMAN. I said nothing to anyone, but the vision was strong and clear, and I wanted to jump all SEVEN STEPS TO HEAVEN to be with her as the drummer cleared the way. I drank one whisky; my lady friend refilled me another. Saying nothing, she knew I was enjoying her album, but she had no idea how much or where it took me.

"I LOVE A CALYPSO, let's dance, Andrei." So, we did. My two friends and their girlfriends followed; everyone considered it an unreserved right watching one another sway, all highly enjoyable; our sense of taste highly flavorful; we didn't know how witty we were, but we were definitely yummy to one another.

Positively the wee hours, and very early morning it was, well after three A.M. All complimented the album and Grace for finding it, yet I found myself not erotically stimulated with the charm and warmth of my lady, because I was overwhelmed with thoughts of another. Together Grace and I shared much, but never did I ever share Maria with anyone, not even with my mother and sister, wondering now, after nearly three more years—eight years since our first meeting—just where was she; how was she doing?

* * *

Quietly, I recalled reading some of her soft but infrequent letters, wishing that she only lived across the state line or that she was somewhere in Germany or Switzerland, or back home for a visit in Zakopane. In her last letter she said that she was thinking of retiring from the pressure of the Big Cat, its demands of performance and travel. She confesses that she was a bit tired and that it was not that unusual for a classical pianist, as for any entertainer, to step down and take a break. After all she had a BS in Biology and loved Botany. In her amusing way, she thought that a National Park Biologist would be perfect; not only for summers, but that no one would know her to chase after just for an autograph. "I could lose myself," she wrote, "and wait for you to come over with your Green Card and together we could help one another again." Her last sentence in her last paragraph ended with "I jokes. Don't you just love it?

    "Miss you,

    "Love, Maria"

        I noticed that she had no return address; a sure sign that she's tying up loose ends. Well, so be it; but what a loose end she is for me, and I for her. Then it dawned on me, I bet she's decided to have a family; she's expecting; what else could it be? I will write to her and wish her well. How wonderful it must be to be her husband. Yet I would not be surprised to find that in her nonchalant manner, she just dropped out of existence for a short while, much like I sometimes like to do when I go to the mountains to just sit and think and plan how to escape my entrapment. But for the moment, I think I'll try to locate her or see if she is connected to an agency who can forward her mail from a fan.

* * *

Computers and the internet were fashionable but not readily available for purchase, for they were costly; and Bulgarians were poor. So poor that we just went to the local coffee house where the machine was made available, but not instantly, for there were few pieces of this new equipment in the country. One had to wait; then one had to be instructed on how to use it correctly. But once I got the hang of it, I enjoyed getting acquainted with the outside world. Thinking of Maria, I decided to try to find out about her performing, and was there a background on her accomplishments. This internet was supposed to give access to anyone, anywhere in the world. Like most amateurs, I began at the bottom.

Then it dawned on me, "Chopin," concert halls, festivals. Under Chopin Competitions in Warsaw, Vienna; going back a few years, I found Maria Kucharski Johnsonn of Chicago, Illinois, the winner of the Polish Piano Festival competition in Warsaw, Poland, capturing the gold medal and thirty-five-thousand-dollar prize at the event. She had awards in Piano from the Kosciuszko Society in New York and the Philharmonic Society of Vienna. Maria Kucharski Johnsonn had given recitals in Japan, St. Petersburg, Russia. Featured soloist with the Chicago Symphony Orchestra, The San Francisco Symphony Orchestra, the Los Angeles Symphony Orchestra and the National Symphony Orchestra in Ningbo, China.

Wow! She's marvelous just like I knew she was. Sitting back in my chair, I was overwhelmed. Knowing I sat with one of the great pianists of the world, and she played expressly for me. No one ever would believe me. What a wonderful memory. Thank you, Maria. God bless you.

*   *   *

But there was another problem for me and my Jazz Club-Bar: inflation. Crazy as it sounds, the bar business was terrific; pay was good and tips were even better. Knowing it was an opportunity that would come and go, I took advantage. Every day I ran to the bank and exchanged my money into American dollars; in no time I bought and paid for a really nice apartment for my mother and sister and I. One problem was now under control, our independence established. But it wasn't long lived; four years later, the mob wanted my bar and me out. I was now 26 and wanting no problems for me and my family,

I simply gave it to them. Had I put up a fuss, insisted on a buyout and held out, my family would be put in jeopardy, or I'd be managed with a bullet or, simply, never be found.

But now I had some good money and found a partner. Together we opened a little green grocery store in the bottom of a basement, but quite visible to the outside and walkers by. It proved to be quite handy to those who needed a head of lettuce, canned articles or toiletries. It was so good that it fed two households for seven years.

Chapter Eight

A Different Job

I've always loved the peaceful enjoyment of Nature, knowing that beneath the soil everything was at work; two hundred years later, full circle, and one square inch of forest soil was properly fertilized, ready for nurturing whatever it was given. Such quiet time made Maria feel complete, providing for good thoughts, reflections and wonderful nights of deep sleep. Ever since she was employed by the National Park Service, she always imagined a tiny piece of property that one day she would find on the border of Glacier Park that someone overlooked and she purchased, for back taxes. And yes, such a dream came true. For it was here in her little refurbished log cabin, she recharged her energies. Sitting and reading extensively amid old silvered logs of many years gone by, Maria knew that each log and book had its own story from one page to another, smiling whenever she recalled the comparison.

The front living room library was her favorite place either before or after breakfast, lunch or dinner or into the early hours of the cool summer mornings. Her little writing desk was near the big picture window facing west. It provided ample light and a mix of deciduous and big healthy pines a few feet from the cabin that were tall enough to cover the great Western mountain peaks of the park. But that was no obstruction, for it gave her great comfort to know everything was in order, standing right behind those big trees. Daily, she hiked the trails, often walking off through meadows and valleys following a whimsical thought, to see a particular wildflower; to find the hoot owl she heard the night before, or to view the peaks of Bear Head and Bison from a different angle, sometimes stepping onto a rock and one more to get a better view of cathedral aisle southwest of the old Lubeck Guard Station.

The other picture window faced south with the same mix of pines and giant cottonwoods on the other side of a makeshift lawn. Inside, opposite the great picture window was a baby grand piano; not the big cat that she was so comfortable with a few years earlier but its offspring, its kitten, silently sitting near the long silvered-log wall with its bookshelves, and memories of a wonderful past that occasionally summoned her to phrase a little of her favorite pieces, nothing grandiose or dramatic, just simple chording now. And in the corner next to the natural rock fireplace was her favorite recliner. This hideaway log cabin near the Midvale creek, Maria loved. From the kitchen window over the sink, while doing dishes, she daily looked out at the Midvale, not more than sixty feet away now finely settled within is fickle banks waiting the next hundred year's flood. Not infrequently did she sneak through the underbrush to her favorite deep, still water fishing hole, neatly carved within the side of the bank, not far up along the creek. Silently, she stands against a big cottonwood; patiently waiting in its shade with pole, line and baited hook for one or two of the nice-size rainbows that she noticed early in the week. Backing away a little, so not to cast her reflection or a shadow in the pond, she watches a beauty meander in to take a look at the wiggly worm that caught his eye; cautiously, swimming around wiggly worm, sometimes talking to himself or to his handsome lady friend, who came along for the swim. Then in a sudden flare of bravado, he snags wiggly; twice as quickly, his lady friend vanishes; and up Maria snags a fresh delicious rainbow dinner.

There are other times by the pond when she just sits and reads or contemplates her existence, and the few guys she's met; her one marriage mistake, now a total blur, and her forestry work. With a miniscule smile of reminiscence, while shaking her head, she recalls a brief encounter that she had just this year when working in the Redwood National Park in Northern California.

Blond hair, a goodly physique and just about six feet, Edward was a very attractive tourist who was insistent on photographing rare floral specimens, which I then confirmed to him its technical name and rarity. Quite often it happened that our group had to wait for him to catch up, but his enthusiasm endeared him to most of us who began to ask him questions, and, in particular, to me. By profession, he was a photographer but not just any photographer; he was a high-fashion photographer whose specialty was to photograph high-fashion models. And the way he told it, he had a very exciting life style, traveling the world: Amsterdam, Paris, Madrid, Florence, and Rome and more than once to Greece then Egypt. And, yes, I did accept his offhand invitation after hours for a little dinner at one of the local diners.

Interesting part was that he married one of his models, Ami. She was only seventeen, and he had to get her parents' permission and signatures to seal the deal, so he wouldn't be accused of robbing the cradle; volunteering that, at the time, he was thirty-five, most definitely, full of himself. One accepted photo in VOGUE he said paid fifty thousand dollars, and, according to him, he was quite prolific; together, his child bride and he lived a glamorous life. Smiling to myself, silently listening, thinking all things, good and bad, come to an end; his was no different.

The two lovers got along well for seven years; that is, he was forty-two and she was twenty-four. Her looks maintained, but her thighs became a little too stout; her arms a little too plump; no longer was she in demand. Seeing that she was Japanese, her added weight lost her photographic sex appeal to the oriental eye. However, she wanted to become a chef, so Edward paid twenty thousand for her entrance to one of Paris' finest culinary school. Ah, now she was on track with a wealthy husband who had made it possible for her to finally find her niche. That Edwards' story ends well goes without saying, his eyes twinkling, saving the best for last.

It wasn't long before Ami caught the eye of a very handsome chef; actually, quite a stud; teasing one another's challenge, it didn't take long until her working school hours extended to working evening hours in and out of the kitchen where the two lovers carried on wild and furious, passionately filling one another all the time anytime.

Wild affairs are quickly uncovered, and Edward gracefully yielded to his competition because he had Ami sign a prenuptial, which was upheld with no hinges such as a mother and children. Too involved in their careers to take the time, furthermore, Edward said Ami was looking from the moment she entered culinary school, and he believed, early on, long before she was blatantly swimming in the pool. So, he kept his earnings; Ami had a few bucks stashed away.

Believe it or not, no longer was the ex-wife cheerless; finding a new side to work along, Ami was now content with her chef de cuisine, now her chef d'oeuvre.

While listening to Edward's story, Maria's thoughts turned to some of the very romantic music of the opera and operettas that began playing in her head; nothing slushy or overly sappy, but good stuff where sentiment never took hold unless you want it to. So you were in charge, and Maria liked it that way—it was Chopinic—where emotions logically give way to sweeter emotions far too out of reach but never gone over the edge, prudently hanging back in the shadows; more often than not, hanging on to the precipice with one hand where she might look back, pause and wonder.

Graciously, our lady thanked Edward who pressed her for a drink and a longer stay, but Maria remembering what one of her college acting friends told her: that to look obnoxiously irritated, one had to imagine he/she was smelling a fart, then looking about to clarify the indignant culprit; that a smell is equitable to garbage, so to the imagination a fart was the perfect match. Seeing the slight scowl on her face, Edward dared not go farther, thanked her for her company and a surprisingly pleasant evening. Returning thanks for an entertaining evening, Maria had no difficulty escaping an obvious wolf; in short, not interested in some flighty hello-goodbye one-night stand. Although, Maria may now have made the transition to a country girl, still she was sophisticated enough to identify a hustler, or a thirsty carnivore, looking for one more drink and another conquest.

*　　*　　*

Quietly, returning to my lodging, I passed the one little offbeat bar where occasionally some good jazz could be heard. Retarding my pace, I stopped to listen to the singer giving a decent rendition of Edmonia Jarrett's "Someone to Watch Over Me." Hearing the lines ". . . seek and ye shall find . . . only man I ever think of with regret . . . he carries the key; put on speed; oh, how I need someone to watch over me."

Tiny tears began to make their way down my cheeks, vividly recalling my departure with Andrei and all that went before. Trying to escape memory, I looked up at the magnificent giants that surrounded me, and longed to return to my cabin hideaway in Glacier, but for some reason, hidden deep within my heart, digression didn't work.

Looking up beyond these towering giants, I could see stars crisp and sharp, perfection beckoning. An owl hooted, clarifying memories of years ago when Andrei and I were sitting at the edge the forest, hiding from the revealing bright light of the moon, ensconced in one another's arms. While talking softly, I could see his handsome face, feel his chest, hear his heart as his arms enfolded me, and the memory of our short time together roused deeper senses of touch; recalling kisses while sitting on the tiny bench overlooking mother's hometown, Zakopane, wondering if Andrei ever heard my thoughts of wishing us alone; a few hours later, the airport and our last goodbye. Then abandon wild heartbeats in Vienna. I felt good, inspired, and warm all over; in my heart no fear of whatever may come. But that was another time, another chapter. And I began to laugh, for what an imagination I possessed. That I was deluged with guys, and I had so many that I couldn't keep track, totally delusional; laughing, I became hysterical.

"That's right, girl," her subconscious spoke aloud. "You go, dear, keep collecting them; I'll keep reminding you of ridiculous grandeur."

"But I feel so strong; so young; so happy."

"Still your favorite thoughts are of that vibrant Bulgarian from Sofiya? And don't deny it. I really liked him too."

From the many corners of her rich memory, given to few humans, Maria often recalled the guy that got away, back into the stream of many fish, yet an outstanding fish. But, as Andrei said, they were of two different worlds.

Lead dancer of the Bulgarian Troupe, a very sensitive, gentle young man of graceful physique with expressive, dark, wishful eyes answering for us to love in Vienna. The boy-man trapped in a decaying land, responsible for supporting his mother and his challenged sister, harboring thoughts of one day coming to America to truly find himself. He was certainly the right guy with the right metal, but it was the wrong time; in reflection, Maria recalled him refined, a prince. But that was then many years ago and now is today.

Chapter Nine

Two Angels

I was working, settling books and getting things arranged for next week. Outside my store window, the corner of Aksakov and Levski was always busy with the hustle of work-a-day lives, running to catch the bus, waiting for the stoplight to change so they can safely cross the street, or shaking their heads disapproval, watching cars race away to the next stoplight. But today was Sunday, quiet, peaceful. That's what Sunday is truly for; a day of rest, visiting family and friends and easy, comfortable lunches.

Hearing a strange yet familiar sound through the open window, I stopped; indeed, a familiar sound; it was a sound I had been accustomed to hearing daily when I was on tour with the dance troupe in Central Europe. Listening to hear from what direction the voices were coming, moving closer to the window, I looked out and noticed a nicely dressed couple looking at a map standing on the corner, obvious tourists, in need of help. Immediately, I ran up the stairs, skipping every other one, and out through the front door, excited that I was once more going to talk to Americans.

"Excuse me," I asked in my best English, "can I be of help?"

"Oh, yes, indeed," looking up, gratefully responded the lady who seemed to be happy for any advice. "We're lost," she said, "we are looking for the downtown area. We arrived late last night, and the cab driver took us to this charming hotel where we stayed the night. We thought it fun to venture out on our own this morning, but I believe we're lost."

"We're definitely lost," confirmed the gentleman, happy to meet someone who spoke English. "Could you help us, we'd be awfully appreciative."

"First, let me introduce myself: My name is Andrei Ivanov."

"Oh, please excuse us, I feel silly; here we're asking you for help and never introduced ourselves. I'm Theresa Stoddard; this is my husband Lawrence Stoddard."

"How do you do," Lawrence shook my hand.

"Let me shake your hand too," Theresa was very appreciative. "There, now I feel more civilized that we have introduced ourselves."

"I have an idea, seeing that it's going to be quite warm today, why don't we come into my store; we'll have a cup of coffee, fresh croissants, and some of my mother's homemade raspberry jam, and you can tell me about your last trip or where you've been so far in a more relaxed environment."

"Wonderful idea," said Lawrence.

"I agree," smiled Theresa, "you lead, we'll follow."

Against their "no, no" pleas, I discarded earlier morning's coffee and set a new pot brewing. Out came fresh croissants made earlier, plenty of good butter and some of Mother's homemade raspberry jam. I just felt good about these two. As we exchanged conversation, I realized they made a very well-suited couple, sincere and concerned about things and people and each other. Surprisingly, they asked where I learned to speak such good English.

I told them I learned a little in high school; then a great deal more when I toured with our National Bulgarian Folk Troupe in Europe during the summers, but most encouragement came from a lovely girl I met from America who was a classical pianist. "I met her in Zakopane, Poland. But she's somewhere else today; perhaps you've heard of her, Maria Johansonn?"

"Oh, yes, Kucharski is her maiden name but she prefers Johansonn, her father's side; she has said that it's easier to pronounce, but then we have no trouble with either name," answered Theresa. "Indeed, she's just a marvelous classical pianist. I believe Chopin is her forte."

"Yes, yes, you're absolutely right. No doubt about her abilities, she's outstanding."

"Lawrence and I heard her play Chopin with the Chicago Sympathy."

"Actually, Andrei, the two of us have heard her play just about everywhere."

"Oh, my, what a wonderful thing is that; almost everywhere? You must have good jobs that permit such time off."

"Actually, we're both retired doctors," volunteered Lawrence. "I believe it was her first year on tour in Vienna during the summer that we heard her give her two première concerts; just wonderful and was she a success; and the following year, again in Vienna, she gave another Chopin evening concert of his Nocturnes and the second was an afternoon concert when she played some of his Mazurkas and encored with his beautiful PRELUDE IN A MAJOR."

"I believe," excitedly interrupted Dr. Theresa, "your Bulgaria troupe was there during her second appearance. I believe both your performances were divided by one in the afternoon and then next day in the evening in the old town square."

"Were you one of the participants?" asked Dr. Lawrence.

"Yes, I was the lead dancer."

"Doing those leaps; marvelous turns," Dr. Theresa perked up, excited, sitting straight up in her chair, eyes bright, alive, "they were so quick, so perfect; oh, yes, yes, now I remember. You were simply marvelous." Turning to her husband who was smiling, "Lawrence, you were quite amazed with his projected animation, how sincere and graceful, how male; remember, love, your comments?"

"I do, I do. So, you are he," Dr. Lawrence rose. "It's our pleasure to meet you."

Both doctors shook Andrei's hand once more, commenting how small were the four corners of the world and its talent.

Immediately everyone became more relaxed, having a common acquaintance in the classical musical world. All thinking how remote is that.

"You know," added Dr. Theresa, "she's from Chicago."

"I'm sure he knows that, my dear."

"I do. And I made a special trip from Zurich just to see her Vienna première. When our troupe was in Vienna the following summer, I saw both her concerts; she's marvelous. I especially loved her evening concert of Chopin's Nocturnes; simply wonderful. And her final encore is always my favorite: the PRELUDE IN A MAJOR; how beautiful is that. Her playing is so filled with such sensitivity that she perfectly conquers her audience. And I am always so moved whenever she plays; it's like I'm sitting next to her."

Checking himself, becoming emotionally lost whenever he recalls Maria. Pausing a moment to gather his thoughts, he continued, but once more his feelings not entirely hidden. "All that was missing was a candlelit salon filled with a few more men than originally were ladies. I would love to be there; I'd love to sit next to her." Not to reveal any of his love for Maria, he stopped, leaving his guest with his wonderful feelings and extravagant thoughts.

"Simply captivating," commented Dr. Theresa, "the entire audience loved her. She gave three encores; after that evening performance in Vienna, whenever she was coaxed for an encore, which was almost always, she ended each with that beautiful A MAJOR PRELUDE, OPUS 28."

"Oh, yes, that one has special meaning for me," Andrei momentarily closed his eyes. Immediately, they were abruptly opened.

"And you first met her in Zakopane, Poland?" Dr. Theresa asked.

"Yes, I did when our Bulgarian Folk Troupe was on tour. I even fell in love with her." Abruptly stopping once more, he smiled; yet he missed Maria and any thoughts, ideas that anyone may have of her other than newspaper clipping; and now he welcomed his new friends more graciously.

"Who wouldn't with such playing?" Dr. Theresa added.

"What a lovely memory, my dear man," said her husband.

"Indeed, it is."

"Do you have any of her recordings?" Dr. Theresa asked.

"No, but I can see what's available on the Black Market."

"Oh, I forget Bulgaria is still locked down. See what's available out there; it's worth a try, Andrei."

"Yes, I'm sure something of hers is available; she's quite well known, internationally too," winked a knowledgeable Dr. Theresa.

"Indeed, I will try; so, where are you from?"

"Seattle, Washington, USA, and recently married for the third time," Dr. Theresa smiled at Dr. Lawrence.

"To celebrate," he continued, "we decided to tour, flying from Seattle, Washington, to Paris to board the Orient Express all the way to Constantinople touring fourteen days."

"Lawrence and I were quite excited seeing the little towns, some eons behind modern time while others furiously working to keep up to maintain their part of the great world community; truly, we were overwhelmed with the varying landscape of the East. Then onward from Constantinople to Sofiya, following the old road that at one time, and still today, connects Constantinople East into Asia and West into Europe."

"Doubt not, Sofiya is still one of the great crossroads of the world, so full of history," chimed Dr. Lawrence.

"That it is; I'm proud to live with that fact."

"And so full of traveler's confidence, we decided to tour Sofiya by ourselves, but quickly got lost as you witnessed this morning."

Dr. Theresa reached for the knife and sliced another nibble off her flakey croissant, buttering it with his mother's delicious raspberry preserves, commenting on how delicious everything tastes. Telling Andrei that throughout their journey the food was excellent, but nothing compares to this raspberry jam.

Andrei beamed pride. "My mother is quite marvelous with everything she does and her cooking is outstanding."

"You know, Andrei, I can't blame this last mishap on my wife because it was my pride, full of flamboyant male confidence, insisting to push ahead by ourselves."

"Yet it was good, my dear; if not for your insistence, we would never have met Andrei."

"And, how true, thank you for the compliment, my lady."

"How nice it is to hear a wife and husband share and compliment each another."

"Believe it, Andrei, we each have had our share of bad marriages," Theresa exhaling, shook her head from side to side and closed her eyes, indicating it was not at all perfect, "and this one we know is right; not only do we agree on most everything, but those things that we do not see eye-to-eye, we work through, giving us a much better understanding and respect for one another."

"So, I've noticed; it's a wonderful trait to see two people in a marriage work together. It's Heavenly."

Instinctively, I prodded mentally not to let this special couple just thank me and go on their way. True, I liked them, and there was something that drew me to them, like I already had known them all my life.

"I have an idea: Why don't the two of you stay at my place for week; I have two bedrooms; it's clean and pleasant. In the morning, you can help me

73

in the store, stocking and facing shelves, some sweeping and cleaning; in the afternoon my partner will take over, and I will act as your personal tour guide in Sofiya. What do you say?"

"That's very generous, Andrei," Theresa once more straightened in her chair; looking at Lawrence then back to Andrei, they nodded agreement, and all three shook hands to seal the deal.

Chapter Ten

Once More

And, yes, I did promise Doctors Lawrence and Theresa that they could pass on my email address, and that I would try to correspond with their Seattle patient, Maria. But soon after my two guests left, my partner and I became very busy; it seemed that everyone walking by, or while waiting to get on and off the bus, had realized that there was this little grocery around the corner. So, my time was consumed in a very pleasant manner: making money. What a delight.

As the doctors had noticed, I had no computer at the house, but I told them that would not be a problem for me to retrieve mail; because the coffee shop was a good getaway, when I remembered. So now I will have a reason to check "my mail" and feel really important, I bragged to them. When we got to the airport, Theresa gave me a big hug and a kiss on the cheek, thanking me; Lawrence shook my hand with a strong hug, both wishing me the best in my quest for a Green Card to the States.

I waited to watch as my two friends walked down the boarding-ramp.

"He's the right one, Lawrence."

"Yes, he is. We did good, darling."

Then they turned, waved back at me; I did the same, and they were gone, end of story.

*　　*　　*

It wasn't for a couple of weeks; I believe it was more like three or more, because my business had picked up considerably. When I finally went to the coffee shop, I just sat and relaxed, enjoying my brew and second guessing my promise to Lawrence and Theresa to correspond with their patient. I had no idea what was her problem only that she was special to them. And, of course, I gave them my word.

Seeing the affection that Dr. Theresa so sincerely, so kindly expressed to my challenged sister, Dora, and how well they got along, I was impressed, touched; for they did not know Dora or my mother from anywhere. I was convinced that these two American doctors were some of the best people I have ever met, and, more than ever, I was super determined to continue my quest for a draw from the Bulgarian Embassy to go to America. Therefore, I continued to read and learn about America from underground newspapers, magazines, and films. How encouraged I felt, thinking what a wonderful time I had had with these two doctors when I realized I needed another coffee, which was just as delicious as the first. Fortified, I called up my email to see what was going on in the real world, and if I had any messages, particularly from their bedridden patient in Seattle, Washington, USA.

After eliminating computer advertisements, there was a letter from the doctors telling me how much they enjoyed Greece and Rome; again, thanking me for a lovely stay at my place, and how happy they were to meet my mother and sister; definitely, they would be remembered in their prayers, and again praying that I get a good draw for my Green Card to America. I smiled, hoping this year I would be lucky. Really, I thought, we were all sad to see them go; they were genuine people.

And then surprised, I saw it and called it up.

76

* * *

Hello, Andrei!

My name is Maria and was told by Doctors Lawrence and Theresa that if I write to you, you will be good enough to write back. Well, I'm doing just that. I sincerely hope that I'm not taking up your valuable time, and if I am, I apologize. Believe me, if you do not respond, I fully understand.

Anyway, if you do write, I promise not to annoy you by writing every day, but once in a while; and if you want to make that time longer, it's okay with me.

Hoping to hear from you,

Thanks,
A Pen Pal

Wow! What a nice letter; but I am not surprised, it's from an American, for who else could be so honest with such a request.

No second thoughts, I decided to write back; besides, I can learn more new words by talking to another American and improve my English grammar. Who knows, I might even get a chance to meet her. That would be exciting.

* * *

Dear Maria,

Your letter came as a surprise to me, even though I was expecting it. I guess we have something in common; we know the same doctors. They are really very good people.

The day they left for Greece, they asked me if I would write to you, if I got the time; I told them that I would, and I see that your letter has been here for quite a few days. Had I known it was here, I would have written sooner. So, please excuse my delay. I am sure they told you that I have no computer at my house, and all my email messages I get from the local coffee shop computer when one is available. But now I will have something interesting to look for instead of just erasing useless advertisements.

Honestly, this is different for me and quite exciting.

77

I hope I'm not boring, and if I am, just tell me. You have the call to continue or not to, and I will understand.

Sincerely,

A Pen Pal

P.S.: I know you are an American. Just in case they didn't tell you, I'm Bulgarian.

Chapter Eleven

Slowly Unfolding

That someone would write to me, how exciting. And his English is good. Just this simple letter gives me the feeling that I'm still alive and viable. Oh, my, I must thank the doctors again when I see them tonight. That they promised to get me someone to write to, talk to, and they did. If my letter writer only knew how happy his words have made me, I bet he would be surprised. That he has given me carte blanche to continue our arrangement or not tells me he's a gentleman, as originally verified by the doctors. That he is a very busy person involved in his business but very honest and "up front." I'll ask if writing to him once every two weeks is satisfactory; that is, I write the first week, and he has two weeks to respond. Then I will do the same, waiting two weeks before I answer him. That's not too intrusive, and I will ask for his input; yes, that will be more amicable for us each.

So, what else shall I tell him; how do I start, really? There's so much to talk about. Oh, I sound just like a lost woman wandering about the desert for the past forty years. And my woman's tribe has just seen their first man. Competition is tough! That's hysterical! Maybe he won't be amused; I certainly don't want to scare him away.

"Okay, Maria," my conscience whispered, "just slow down. You don't want to overwhelm him, dominate him; after all he's just a pen pal. Get a grip, girl; go easy, rein in the horses, restrain yourself. You're not removing all constraints. Definitely, your legs

are properly crossed; you're just writing a letter to him, telling him a little about yourself,
and you go from there, girl, gently, easily. Remember you're not conducting a marathon,
yet I know you wish you could; and it's not an intellectual marathon; it's simply a meet-
ing of two people through a letter, words on a piece of paper. Remember this isn't 1806
where you're writing to a Mountain Man on the upper Missouri from St. Louis. For
certain, you can handle it. Then it took mail sixty days to half a year or more to get to
the guy whereas today it's words on a computer delivered in a matter of seconds right
to his page, halfway 'round the world. Think of it this way: It's as simple and quick as
transposing from the key of F # to C major. It's just like a blind date. Furthermore, he
may never see you; you may not be here that long. Got it, girl?"

"Thanks for reminding me. I got it."

So, I sent this guy an informative note telling him about my family, my
sisters and a little about my educational background, but not any of my musical
accomplishments. I was afraid that I might slip, and give him the impression
that I'm bragging, now feeling sorry for myself or that he might feel that way
toward me.

This was the beginning, and how true a first date, more like a touch-and-
go. I also sincerely thanked him for taking the time to write me, and that I
hope I'm not a bore in what I have to say. Eagerly, I awaited his reply, wanting
to know just what kind of business he had, and how things in Sofija were.

*   *   *

We carried on just as Maria suggested writing and returning a letter every
two weeks or so; it was convenient and really no bother for either of us, furthermore, I would have updated information of what was going on with the
business and my life, my interests, her interests. At best sometimes two letters
per month or maybe just one, subject to our free time and my business, for it
was becoming more and more demanding with daily new and repeat cus-
tomers, and so thankful that I had not rushed into a daily or weekly correspondence. But I did thank her for increasing my business, albeit unknown to her
and to me.

Smiling to myself, thinking, I bet she would think I'm a little loony that
my business has continued to steadily grow, since the two doctors and now
talking to her. Anyway, it has, remarkably!

Then I remember mentioning that I had taken a self-taught photography course by one of Ansel Adams successful students. I told her how much I loved the course; loved photography, and that I really learned quite a bit. Whenever I got the chance, to the mountains I went to photograph flowers, odd formations, mountain scenery and wildlife. Photographing wildlife taught me patience to be successful. For every time I went back into the mountains, I would fall in love with some of my wondrous opportunities with Nature; how beautiful and mutable was her garden; wildflowers blooming and changing at every altitude during the seasons in the high country. How light and gay were the spring flowers; mellow and stalwart those blooms under the long hot summer's sun, and the fall was always an array of deeper, stronger hues in preparation for cool nights and early snowy morning. Nature was marvelous at survival, making sure things fit and so attractive.

As she, herself, was a biologist with emphasis in botany, Maria was quite impressed and could appreciate my efforts in planning and timing. I asked her if she wanted to see some of my photos, and, yes, she did indeed.

I mailed her about eight that were taken in the summer and the last of some our deep-purple fall mountain flowers, high in the Balkans, primarily in the Rila mountainous area. And would you believe it, she identified them all, including their Latin genus; like the Genus Castilleja, Indian paintbrush; Erigeron glabellus, Smooth Fleabane, with its fine leaves circling its deep yellow-brown center sun; and the delightful Chrysanthemum leucanthemum, the Daisy. I was quite surprised, to say the least; I was impressed.

I continued sending photographs of my outdoor haunts, my place of work and the area where I live, which is one of the most beautiful places in Sofia.

*   *   *

By Christmas we had exchanged about five or six letters, beginning sometime in the middle of September, and we were establishing a comfortable writing relationship. We did mention that our faith was similar; Catholic and Greek Orthodox. And that was the extent of our religious involvement.

Because business was so good, continuously my letters were short. And there were a few times that I missed the two-week spacing. Everything quite literally racing away; when I wrote again, it was June 2004. Sincerely apologetic,

I blew away any kind of decorum when I dared to write, asking if she were ever married—can you believe that I was so bold; or should I say curious, that sounds more polite, but nosey sounds correct.

She did respond by telling me that she was once married, and it was all very awkward; nothing was really good about it because she had rushed into it, not thinking good or bad of the future just the immediate situation. That she was emotional, yes, to say the least; but that I should not think that she was unstable just immature at the time, then asked me the same in return.

Seeing what she said was exactly what had happened to me, I told her everything just fell apart, realizing that there was more to a marriage than just sex.

Also, I slowly continued to crack any remaining ice between us by asking why was she so long in the hospital. I've never heard of tests taking so long; did she go home in between tests or was this something new, or were her tests, possibly, experimental; and was she a volunteer?

Maria wrote back mentioning nothing of her hospital or her experiments, but asked me if I had any fond memories that I might like to share; perhaps a favorite; she would do the same.

I wrote back telling her that I had two such favorite memories; one was my love of photography, of which she was already quite aware. But then I really let lose, for I was "bursting to tell her," as they say in America, that I was also crazier for another love; one in which I really excelled: folk dancing and the one special person I met.

Dear Maria:

I hope you do not find this hard to believe, but it was not more than a few years ago when I was the lead dancer of our Bulgarian Folk Troupe that traveled throughout Europe. Actually, we were ambassadors, representing our country. But after our engagements were fulfilled, we return home, for we do not have any dance touring companies that perform like they do in Hollywood, California, or on the Broadway stages in New York City. Alas, we're just simple but talented Bulgarians confined to our country, let loose only during summers. And when we toured Europe, we had many wonderful experiences, and met many wonderful people, mostly tourists, especially those from America. And, Maria, I have many wonderful stories to relate; some very precious memories that will live with me forever.

One in particular, was of a wonderful pianist I had the pleasure of meeting, spending a little time with her and her two American girlfriends and family in Za-kopane, Poland. It was just a beautiful occasion. She took us to a place called the Tram-polina somewhere in the Tartra Mountains. It was quite interesting as the entire building bounced up and down when the crowd inside was dancing; hence the name Trampolina. We danced, had a few drinks, socialized; then she and I went outside and just sat quietly on the porch railing and talked, danced a little. We then moved out to walk about the surrounding area; still faintly hearing the music, again we danced a little on a large maintained lawn; then found a big bold old log on the out-skirts of the forest where we comfortably settled ourselves and continuing talking, get-ting to know one another.

Then for a change of scenery, we had moved to the bench overlooking the town of Zakopane. Everything was just marvelous; music had faded in the distance, then silence. It was picture perfect. But it wasn't long before her two friends came out to get us.

Are you at all familiar with this place? Silly question, I know; I'm sure you're not; then maybe you are; if you were, I know that you would love it. At one time it was a tiny village that now slowly grows up.

Another time I remember hearing her play Chopin, her specialty, when she ap-peared in Vienna one year later at her première. She did remember me, but her agent kept a close rein on her and on her schedule. Although we did shake hands and shared a quick embrace.

The following year, she was again in Vienna giving a two-day concert, one in the evening and one in the afternoon. Fortuitously, on the second evening, we bumped into each other at one of the refreshment tables. Quickly, we sneaked away down a narrow side street into one of the tiny cafes around the corner. Even though we exchanged ad-dresses, we never corresponded; soon I got my letters returned—no forwarding ad-dress—and that was that, but she was exceptionally talented. Never heard from her again. I'm sure she moved on, got married, but she was quite a gifted pianist to say the least. I have read of some of her accomplishments. Then, again, who was I to com-mand such talent.

Honestly, I'm still in love with her, but it was never meant to be. Strange when I recall, it was as if it all happened in a moment in time then gone. I have never heard of her since; although, I have finally found a few of her Chopin albums, thanks to Doc-tors Theresa and her husband, Lawrence, who followed her career. Truly, that is my most precious memory. Believe me, she was not just exceptional; she was brilliant, gifted, and I believe she is somewhere, probably, living in New York playing Chopin concerts to select audiences. Seeing that you live in Seattle, I doubt if you know her, although, I wouldn't be surprised if you knew of her.

So, now you know I have experienced some interesting things in my life rich to recall, and, as they say in New York, so, how's by you?

Your Pen Pal

* * *

Oh my God, my intuition was right. Slowly, nervously I put down his letter, for it was almost impossible for me to believe. Then I read it again. He is Andrei, my Andrei, lead folk dancer of his Bulgarian Troupe. He's back! He's back! Oh, this is crazy; this is madness; I'm all a flutter, delirious with the thought of holding him once more, loving. Oh, my God, I'm so happy; I could scream for joy that it's he. I know that it's he. I gotta get a hold of myself, yet this feeling is so wonderful; but I don't want to get too far ahead of myself. After all, it's been eight years since we first touched and talked, kissed and loved; now, looking back, it feels like all was yesterday. When I think of his arms about me, I grow weak, my heart quickens at the thought of us together once more. Oh, my God, my God.

If only I can forget my pain; if only I can embrace him; oh, my heart beats so fast, so loud it sounds like drums of the world racing to great him; if only I could run ahead of that beat. I know I'm right, though; I know it. I loved him first at the Zakopane festival then lost him; found him the next year for a handshake and a brief hug in Vienna, but the following year we found each other once again in Vienna where, without hesitation we ran away and loved the night only to depart for obligation's sake. But now he's here, he's here. Oh, thank God. My brightest memory and the only one whom I let sit next to me while I played for him a private concert. He's the only one. And if it were not for Chopin, I would not know how to contain myself with my wild sophomoric silliness. Oh, how I've missed him. Can this be possible? Oh, please, please, no tricks. In this whole wide world, how can this be happening? My God, what have I done to deserve this; yet no way can I figure this out any more than can I stop my crying for joy. We were only together for a little less than thirty hours including the time he saw my concert in Vienna; then later that second evening, after his troupe's performance, we met at the refreshment table, hurried away to talk then closed the door together . . . . All lost I thought until now, reborn, alive and well once more.

But I can't let him know what's happened to me, yet I cannot keep it a secret. He will find out; already he asks about my tests in the hospital, and I'm surprised he took this long. Perhaps he's just being polite, and that's so like him. Oh, Andrei, my strength, if only you knew how I have missed you, to hold you once more in my arms. Oh, what delight await us. How true is it that love is the heart beat of the world, the universe!

*   *   *

So how do I begin this letter to my love? I'm sorry for the slower than usual correspondence? We've exchanged a few email letters but no phone calls. Nothing until now, and I know you haven't a clue who I am. So, what shall I do? How do I approach this dilemma, this paradox, this definite contradiction? Never should this have happened; it's all unintelligible, incoherent. Quite honestly, I'm on the end of the line, hooked, caught like a fish in my own pond. Save for my excitement, I'm so docile, yet I cannot deny that I'm not unhappy, but just look at me.

I'm a total mess, totally dislodged, immobile and growing worse by the hour. My fingers are useless; my limbs slowly emaciating, so I cannot do anything without help. Yet my mind is completely operable; I can think, I can still talk, but no longer am I beautiful in possession of a body that's presentable, appealing to him; and who knows how long I have to live. Oh, Andrei, don't you ever pity me. Simply turn away and leave me; it's my prerogative, my request, for am I no longer your youthful, beautiful and talented Maria; I'm just an embarrassment. And when you see me, you will fully understand why I never wanted to reveal myself through our letter exchanges, verbally or photographically. And now that I know it's you, most of all you, my love, consider yourself lucky we lost contact.

If you are here, oh, God in Heaven, give me strength to handle this encounter. For no longer am I able to endure rejection, especially from my one and only love.

It took me days to regain some composure. When I did write back

85

telling him that I was once married, but, right from the onset, it was an unhappy marriage, stormy; nothing was right, and we soon parted, happily, most of all, for me. And that was all I wrote, fearing too much possible revelation of feelings if I spoke or mentioned Zakopane or anything to do with music.

*　　*　　*

Finally, some movement; some revelation of life, revealing actions, making her persona less a mask, less mysterious; a little more an author consenting to some interesting insights, deeds. Happy to get her mail and she is interested in talking about other things, herself and her life. That was good, and I wrote back.

Maria,

I too was once married and have a baby girl now about 9 years old, living in England with her mother. Mother and daughter are doing well, but I never see them, rarely ever speak to them; and I mean never on both accounts.

So, Maria, do we want to see what similarities we might have between our two fallen marriages? It might give us better ground to understand each other and maybe open ourselves for equal examination, making us more successful when next time it comes around; as I'm sure it will for each of us.

May I be so bold to ask how "hunting" in America is; you know, guys and girls looking for and dating other guys and girls, or are second marriages frowned upon? I'm just curious, nosey, more like trying to make interesting conversation in another direction. What do you have to say about that?

If you've done any homework, you know that I'm stuck here in Bulgaria half a world away, but we are close to the same latitude or somewhat close. Because our country is not yet part of the European Union, every year I have to put in my name to the Bulgarian Embassy to see if I get picked to go to America.

Do you know that we've been communicating for almost a year now? What have you to say about that?

Also, I'm going to purchase a computer, so I do not have to run down to the coffee shop. I'm sure you agree that it's a good idea?

Seeing that neither of us has ever signed his complete name, don't you think it's about time we should?

Pen Pal
Andrei Ivanov

*   *   *

Dear Andrei,

You know, I believe that I know you; how's that for a grand opening, just a little crazy? I've been thinking to myself quite a bit, and, yes, I believe that it's time that you get that computer; make sure it has terminals for Skype because I want to see you, and I want you to see me. Write me when you have things set up. If you need any help financially, let me know because I want to help you—no obligations, ha, ha; and just how do you fulfill my kind of obligations half a world away like marriage or trips over to America. You're safe with me, for I'm stuck here for some time now; but I will tell you more when we can see each other over Skype.

Then see how many new words you will learn to speak, read, and write. Already you have a wonderful grasp of the English language, but I will take great joy in helping you expand your linguistic dynamics.

Until then, Love,
Your Maria

*   *   *

Oh my God, how did I not know it was she? I'm a guy. But that's a terrible, yet an honest excuse.

Memories past recreate a sense of the moment as I recall the two of us talking at the Trampolina, holding one another as we slow dance, expressing the urgency of our nearness, yet wholesome. I was twenty-one; she twenty-two. One year later in Vienna, a handshake and a hug; the second year we finally let our expressions go, and now pass eight more years; oh, what have we lost that is now found, but better later, for still it's never too late. And a more realistic and colorful word picture we share with the magic of modern technology. How is this meeting possible and all the while writing to each

87

other and now revelation? What beauteous miracles life holds for us? How I long to see her to be with her, my Maria. My heart beats faster at just the thought of once more being with her; I believe I cannot say that I'm not a little overly excited.

Chapter Twelve

What to Expect

I feel like I'm making my first appearance, and, well, yes, it is, silly girl that I am, and I want to look my best. Yet it has been ten years since our first touch; in truth, eight years since we last loved. Still, it's a first time and womanly worries naturally pervade, especially my appearance: *Is it good; is it bad; do I look attractive, not too circumspect with the awkwardness of my sickness. Do I look feminine? Will he like what he sees? Will he like me long enough to engage conversation, and I wonder what we will have in common to discuss? Will he have even half an ember for me; I wish too much.*

Oh, this is like television; everything has to be just right. So different from just writing an email; with an email we can imagine what each looks like.

Intuitively, she realized from Andrei's talk of the pianist from Zakopane that the two Angels never revealed to her that it was Andrei from Sofija, giving her the joy of making her own discovery. Well, here goes.

Words racing emotional madness, utter surprise surging capture of her true love once again; miraculously, she moves slightly upward, momentarily out of her sitting position, with her cry of "Andrei!"

She's alive, contemporary; a songstress of the latest most outrageous melodies, expressions, movements; Maria's lovely, beautiful; she's in love. And there's nothing she cannot do. She's a show stopper: She dances, she moves, she's graceful. The essence of every man's dreams, yet reserved only for one man's sweet love, the man she's bound to, her Andrei. Yet our princess is barely holding on, at best, just holding on, surviving from day to day, but today she's going somewhere.

I will open up only to someone I can trust. He will know everything, everything about me. I've decided to hide nothing, so he can honestly see and evaluate whether to stay or to go away, and if he leaves, so he does, and I won't blame him. For who can deny him, to lie to keep him is terribly unjust;

Yet I'm bound to him now. It's that same wonderful safe feeling that I felt before—but now our circumstances, our distance between us—physically; yet it is beyond the thoughts of the ordinary human to grasp. Oh, I'm so giddy; I can walk across a tightrope; dance on a pinhead. I'm feeling wild, out of control; acting and thinking silly, of course I'm in love. Again, twirling my finest pirouettes, while walking down Michigan Avenue. The Gold Coast is outrageously beautiful at this time of year, and so am I because I'm in love, surrounded with melodies of passion, for I'm seeing Andrei. I close my eyes and ask the nurse for a hand mirror, and there I am: warm then hot, flushed, through and through; it's freezing temperatures in my hometown, Chicago, but I don't care because I'm in love. I so want to explode; never to shift into overdrive to save fuel, for what? Need to hurry to make out with my love; and I'm hotter than any star, for I am the star, shaking and crying all at the same time. Oh, who cares? Once more the lost is found.

*   *   *

Through the magic of computer technology, I see my Maria for the first time since Vienna, eight years ago. Never before have I seen such beauty radiating warmth and love from 12,000 miles away. Never expecting to see her again, I am stunned; and there she is right before me, clear eyes, red hair; her sweet smile, proof positive that she is Maria. And I'm struck with the thought that God made her, exclusively for me and once more together. Literally, pinching myself, I begin to tear, knowing that I love her more than the first time; more than ever before, now forever.

"Hi," impatiently she calls out like some eager teenager, making contact with her new boy toy.

"Maria, can you see me because I can see you very clearly. You look marvelous, Maria."

"And you're a sight for sore eyes," as we say here out West in America.

"How can this be, Maria; it's a miracle." Beside myself, I stammer; I cry my tears to complement hers; silence, whispering, hesitating for all is blur except for Maria before me on the screen half a world away; suddenly nothing matters anymore because I am home; unabated our tears flow freely while each perceives the other with great moisture.

Astonished, as if we are dreaming, still she is more striking than ever. A butterfly so delicate, so alive; I hesitate. As we talk, I become more aware that Maria is stationary; all movement is no movement; she's static in gesture; she's immobile. Something is not right.

Yet Maria is anything but quiet, and that's good, for I love to see her active, even if it's highly confined.

For two souls who crave conversation that only they can grasp and enjoy is priority to our human bondage.

Once again subtle conversation, romantic, poetic and operatic, that only we two lovers in the sphere beyond can appreciate and deeply comprehend of how old things are forever new. Yet all is equal for once more we have each other. At last, all is complete just as art imitates Nature; but once again, rarely seen in human form, Nature now imitates art.

Gone deceptive illusions; once again lovers together rekindle erotic imaginings. At last, we have no impediments; no opposition only love and truth. For truth is love's cornerstone of goodness for life's perpetual pleasure; foremost, the lead step to happiness on Earth. And so, my Butterfly has captured her Pinkerton.

Later, when again I saw her, I couldn't refrain talking to myself with great joy, her nurse by her side assisting her:

I love this quiet time watching her trying to position herself as if she's getting ready for an interview or a gentle conversation of love. So fragile and delicate is she that I think she'll break in two.

Leaning toward the screen, looking into one another's eyes, I remember his first touch, our first kiss, that lover's night in Vienna, naturally, we extend our hand; fingers to the screen to touch each other, as Shakespeare's holy palmers do, and we begin:

"Hi" or "good morning" from my side or "good evening" from hers.

* * *

"Hello, Maria, I love you; I wish you were here." We continue talking right where we left off yesterday for already too much time has been wasted and must somehow be retrieved, even though we are better than half a world away, for she is no longer in New York, but at the far Northwestern end of America, Seattle, Washington.

Yet the world continues churning, turning, creating life and business, laborers, jobs, high-rises filling up; couples all over planning, living, loving: cafes full with morning and afternoon gatherings; evening parties in bars, clubs; assignations at every hour of the day, or just simply at home. All this we talk about over Skype longing for one another in absentia; each trapped by confines inhuman. But we are happy to be talking and dating; crude as it is, yet it is a marvel of technology that makes us possible again, sharing thoughts and distant love, always longing for a better sharing of real physical tangibles: holding hands, touching each other, your fingers through my hair or mine through yours, wishing just once more for two bodies to embrace, hearts to merge as one ardent fire; and always just one more kiss. Yet we are sharing all the same; poetically, the image is soothing, but now our images are forever, yearning, documented, recalled for future generations. Do I really want all that?

Yes, yes, I do. If there were only some one special place where I could take her to heal; some enchanted forest where the well is deep-hidden; its water magic-healing and the wind through tall pines regenerates spirit, soul, new life and happiness given. She will be reborn; together we will be reborn.

"Maria, I know I've mentioned it before, but I've never forgot about us."

"You're married?"

"Was, now she's gone; and you?"

"My music coach."

"Divorced or still hanging on?"

Maria chuckled with a little snort and emphasized: "Divorc'd."

"And are we lost?"

"Thought so; not anymore."

"Good to hear."

"Really, who wants me, Andrei?"

"I do."

Susceptible I crave so like before
Intense his touch, sweet sensations and more;
Rips passion's cloak, unveils sweetest delight
Unbridled love, ecstasy's sweetest night.

Chapter Thirteen

And More

Be it a mile or a billion miles away over the screen, to them their love was more than tangible. It was real. For they were spiritually wedded; connected in a manner that few humans ever are, whether they be newlyweds, lovers, or luxuriant couples of infatuated exuberances in some hotel room, the back or front seat of an old or new car, or flesh to flesh on the sands of some remote tropical island, alone. Their love was a gift of the Angels, a gift blessed, unique; for it was they who brought them together from the very first time.

"The joy of virgin forests, a new country scented with spring's variegated wild, roguish flowers, full of passion's intensity, favorite scents of Olympian antiquity, their pristine world made perfect for us to love. Oh, Maria, I cry for love of you."

"And my heart yearns for you, Andrei; yet, despite our deep hidden plans, we cannot be together. The walls of my confinement restrict me never on my own to venture. Dependent on others for help, I am firmly locked, caged like a bird and cannot get out for my sickness captures me, cripples me, numbers my days. Sequestered, I have a busy life full of medical successions, costly busy nothings they are. Everything's being done to improve my conditions, they say. They think I'm nothing but a fool, I know I'm captured; I know there is nothing that can be done, save for involuntarily volunteering for another stem cell operational experiment; another needle and deeper, sharper knifes. They have opened

Pandora's Box; their brilliant ideas costing millions to make someone more millions with a new breakthrough or another minute observance amounting to nothing, not even a footnote in the Multiple Sclerosis Medical Journal. After such experimental exhaustion, I feel good for a day or two, but for me nothing good continues; all non-sequitur, except death. Who cares of the cost; I'm a government employee with good insurance, perfect for experimentation; for whatever they do Uncle Sam pays. Results are never satisfying, rarely is anything ever discovered; more like thoroughly bungled, and then some new impairment. Believe me, I cannot get out for the life of me, pulsing, squirming mentally is no adventure; no one but God can set me free. Now that I have met you again, even though it be on Skype, I feel more alive, yet more caged than ever, how cynical is that. You represent a glimmer of happiness and false hope as once before where our two lives came together but could never become permanent to live and love as lovers do. But I love you more than ever, and, once more, I am happy for our limited time. Funny, I must now beware of fainting, loss of control, not for romantic concerns or its wild pornographic indulgences, but for medical concerns over which I have no control. I love you for finding me; I love you as a woman loves a man, deep, passionate, so remote where only souls can communicate. Andrei, you are my only touch with reality, my sense of self, my hero."

"Maria, you are my only real love, truly my heroine. So aligned are we, so removed yet nearly on the same latitude where only true lovers meet. You talk like you play with passion, poised, and filled with love, ravaged with romance, all its senses. Oh, that you were here, that I were there to consummate our longing."

"Oh, Andrei, so often I feel like a child and must have help with everything I do; a caged test animal, a guinea pig, poked and prodded, rolled back to the room and plugged in just for survival for another hour, the next day, if lucky. Oh, love me; love me like a child. Right now, you are my strength, my light; you make me so happy again; though I cannot respond beyond a smile and conversation, but happy I still have my faculties—my mind—and adjoining similar things, subsets like hearing and feelings. Now I am accustomed to little things, soft and gentle, nothing robust for I may crack and fall away. Oh, talk to me, I do respond; I do so want to touch you, once more, again and again, for I miss you so much. I cry for the image, the memories, and the sweet scent of it all:

Mountain's love melting snow, so clear and fresh;
Laughing creeks, alpine showers waken Earth's
Blooms stretching new to meet sweet summer's sun;
Handsome pines surround new leafy green trees.

Relax mind and body; how well I sleep.
My days behind and now I think of him;
The boy I met once who stayed far away;
Tricks again playing in my mind, dancing

Round, now slow, allows me time to focus:
No drums, no fuss only soft sensation;
No sound, no temptation, color abounds,
Whispers from another world's devotion.

Transcend I slowly to another place
Remain spellbound in nature's state of grace.

Chapter Fourteen

Joys of Being Alive

"Those pictures of you and your friend on top of the mountain; how I wish that it were I standing next to that mighty tall cottonwood and you photographing me, partially clad, fully clad or in all my natural elegance. Oh, I'm so jealous, and yet so happy for you and your mother together picking ancient, naturally fresh wild raspberries warmed by the sun; and her telltale red fingers from plucking those irresistible, edible morsels. What camaraderie; how delightful; how delicious devouring them like many enjoyed eons before; oh, how sweet is that.

"If only I could be there with you, alone, just the two of us sitting together, relaxing in each other's arms at the top of your mountain, Vitosha, overlooking our kingdom of Sofija and Great-Great-Grandfather Ilia's estate. Oh, how I wish, how I wish I were there with you before, then and now, but I will have to settle for us over Skype. Goodnight, my love. My fever grows for you, for us, even though I'm confined; but my mind always imagining pictures us, and how happy are we together. Our fingers' kiss, lovers reluctant extend to touch goodnight."

* * *

Maria and I talk every day; each is always special, often quite creative, instructive of how to proceed when I come to America; ideas flow daily, fresh, wholesome with enthusiasm, giving me new ideas to think about, what to look for, and the many opportunities in anthropology, archeology, and how film and the camera is all so important in recording accurately for posterity. Now I smile whenever I think of her initial response about us writing to each every two weeks or so, if we have the time; so cautious was she not to offend or be too demanding for conversation from the outside world. Never did she realize that her two doctors, Theresa and Lawrence, would become such good friends of hers, like mother and father; and how wildly imaginative was their preferred choice of me, surreal.

I concluded that had to be a story all its own; and I gave it a great deal of thought, but until I had more convincing evidence, I kept the thought silent. After all, I didn't want Maria ever to think that I was some kind of nut, imagining thoughts and things that may be consider occult—then again, I believe, her specific situation provides her uncanny insight, or is it supernatural? Often, I think that she has an inside line that is above nature and its laws, beyond surreal, mystical. Then again, all thoughts and idea are always open to her.

Always ahead of the game, my lady is always thinking. And most dearly, I love that about her; it so enhances her beauty. How many times I marvel that had I had two lifetimes, still could I never rival such prescience. So much we enjoy our dialogue, typically spontaneous on any given theme un-prescribed, unprepared, unique; somewhat like Chopin's spontaneous improvisation, hardly; I know, I know; yet intellectually somewhat the same with its splurge of ostentatious intellectual extravagance; its lyrical and gracious logic, or, shall I say, syllogistic order.

Believe me, my lady is no small drop; although darling and dainty she makes quite a splash. Maria plunges right in, and we are off and conversing, always looking at me as though we are right next to one another in the same room each stimulating the other's pulse, sensing the other's touch, both happy and sad; other times with such intensity, it's as though we are getting ready to exchange vows to physically consummate our love.

*   *   *

"Andrei, for once I'd like to be adored; just to feel what it's like. All I can remember is when we first met, and how it felt for me. So, what were your first feelings towards me? When you were sitting next to me in the cafeteria, next to me on the piano bench?"

"But Maria, you must realize that for me it was much earlier."

"Really?"

"It was just before we first introduced ourselves at the table in the basement cafeteria at St. Constance, I did not know what to say. Truly, I was spellbound, already that had taken hold as we were walking down the conclave."

"You mean all that time just before we sat down.

"Yes."

"Oh, my," Maria blushed crimson, and I could see her complexion growing darker and darker, especially when she vainly made an effort to raise her hand to cover her face.

"And sitting next to you when I heard you play, so close to you; it was over. And how I wanted to touch you, to be part of your goodness; for proof, I remember asking myself, 'Where do I sign?' I was a done deal in the bottle caught and capped. All I wanted was to be with you forever. So, now you really know. And the rest of the evening was a dream for me. And when you looked at me and kissed me at the kitchen table in you aunt's house, just before our 4 A.M. breakfast, I knew, for sure, that you too were captured."

"But we had never slept together, so how could you know the culmination?"

"Sometimes, my dear, feeling is intuitive. And the rest is just magical follow through that each knows is going to be perfect no matter how or when it occurs. Perhaps it was the intervention of Saint Constance, the patron saint of the parish."

"You know of her origin?"

"A little. She was the daughter of Constantine the Great, the first Christian Emperor—325 A.D.—of the Roman Empire; by his decree fifty million inhabitants under his rule became Christians. Except I needed no official order for me to love you, I just did."

"Well, Andrei, thanks to you, I now know what it feels like to be adored. And, if you please, let me tell you how I first felt."

*　*　*

"For me everything began just a little earlier when I was part of the audience watching your troupe perform. Actually, you were wonderful; you were really in charge. And when I saw you solo, I was amazed, for never had I witnessed anyone so full of inspiration, so vibrant with such energy. You were fire, a spirit, like something down from Olympus, and the audience was well aware of it all, especially you. Your leaps, were all higher than most dancers were supposed to achieve, and your turns, snapped attention and focus. You thrilled everyone. I thought you were larger than life. Just watching you perform gave me goosebumps."

"Really?"

"Really, my love! When we were walking and talking down the conclave to the cafeteria, I felt as if I were in a danger zone; but you were not the danger; it was I. Never had I ever felt that way before; though we were young, even now when I recall those moments, I still hope you didn't notice that besides my obvious goose bumps, I slightly stuttered. All unplanned, nothing prompted, and I thought:

"It's coincidence. Then hearing my father's voice: Remember, Maria, nothing ever happens without a plan; too easy, too irresponsible to relegate these things to accidental happenings or to chance. There's so much goings on in the universe, we humans do not understand, think of, let alone even imagine; we are part of great powers; we are the free-spirited reproductive elements of those powers, like the free radicals of a burning candle; free thinking creative individuals. Relax my child; see what happens; go on, chance it. Maybe he's a fluke. And his voice was gone.

"We continued walking, inadvertently slowing, but I never felt that I wanted to get away from you. I was caught off guard, cornered, corralled; my breath you took away. You noticed? Of course, you noticed."

"I noticed that we talked; but you said very little, almost nothing, and then we reached the table."

"Where Donna Rae and Pricilla definitely made up for my silence."

"True. But I too was really taken with you, and I knew nothing about you yet."

102

"I was amazed that you were so natural; so unassuming. I loved you right then, Andrei, and somehow, I thought, perhaps somewhere before, too. Furiously, I was trying to be cool, collecting my wild thoughts now gone topsy-turvy, down the mountainside, more like trying to pull a broken top over a convertible while the rain only gets heavier and you get wetter; there's no escaping, you're caught.

"I told myself that it was all silly. He's a foreigner; you're a foreigner, but his English is amazing. You spoke it well, honestly. And I kept getting flashes throughout my body, rising up to my skin, hoping that I was not showing that I was blushing hot for you, an unencumbered first, I want you to know. Never before had such explosive feelings come to me; always too busy, practicing, rehearsing—always was I pristine and careful, and, if such feelings did arise, truly, I was unaware; but not, then, when walking with you; sitting with you, talking to you. My mind was telling my body: Maria, you are not in control because in this situation no one is, and you are exploding from the inside out; soon everyone will know about you and him.

"When we sat at the same table, I was surprised, for I thought you would excuse yourself to find friends of your troupe and leave us to be with them. I was glad when you stayed."

"Maria, I was magnetized to you; yet we were both very reserved; you more so than I. And was I pleased; it gave me time to compose myself. I knew you were special, but first I had to be quiet, to somehow figure you out; just who were you; why was I so attracted to you, and why were you so special? Why? And why right then was everything converging on me; and why was this happening to me?"

"I believe you had girlfriends before, for you were quite personable in appearance and attractive; your talents were marvelous, you were a leader."

"Yes, I had girlfriends, but never like you. Right away you were special. And I was just drawn to you; I couldn't figure anything other than I knew that you were exceptional. Something just kept telling me so."

"Donna Rae and Pricilla thought you were 'hot,' and they too realized that, besides their feelings and thoughts for me and you, something was brewing between us. On the return flight to London and back to New York, you were their main topic. They said when I was with you, I never hid a thing. Were my emotions that blatant?"

"If they were you hid them well when we were having dinner. After dinner when we walked down the hall to the stage, I sensed that you liked me. And when you began to play, I just wanted to be near you."

"When you came a little closer, my heart began to race, but I was determined to play for you, whatever my instructor said. And I began."

"I loved how you slowly warmed up rarely looking at the keys yet you knew where each finger was going."

"Of course; that comes with much practice."

"And great talent, my dear Maria, but I haven't finished, continuing to make you feel adored?"

"Yes, continue, no more interruptions, I promise. I love when you talk to me this way. There is so much to remember, but most of all I remember the way you touched my cheek then kissing it, and how we grew so intimate from there on the piano bench, no shame."

"Neither was there for me, my dear, for such love knows no guilt; and boldly right in front of Donna Rae and Pricilla we performed."

"And all those who were silent in the back of the little theatre, slouching and loving in the dark last rows, Andrei."

"Listening and enjoying while you were playing."

"Already was I that much in love with you. I didn't care; I was proud of my feelings, no shyness because I felt so secure just being with you; and I knew right then I'd never love like this again. I just wanted to be with you. And now look at us. No shame in this, my love."

"No, there isn't, Maria. And such music I never heard played before; played with such sensitivity, consummate maturity, shifting tones, shading the softest, most delicate of feelings; settling to depths unknown, stirring the distant ends of our finest, forsaken emotions. I was hearing a rebirth of a nation, an emergence of its culture, fresh and totally new. I felt with you that I could do anything. You were marvelous then, and you are more marvelous now, my dear."

"On the porch at the Trampolina when we kissed once more, Andrei, I was all fire, but you controlled yourself and gently checked me. And I loved you for your self-control, and so enjoyed the warmth of your arms about me. You then told me that I was beautiful, and I loved you for it; so sincere; my God, I loved you.

"Don't change a thing, I thought; just keep sitting next to me, for that is when I'm most susceptible to you. Yet how scared was I; everything was so new; then gently all fear disappeared; the Coastal mist revealed its vision, and I knew you were the one. That we were a match; and I knew we would be together again; I was sure of it.

"Oh, Andrei, thank you. Later, I'll tell you what happened to me, but now I'm enjoying our loving compliments, and, for now, that's where I want to be, where LOVE NEVER ENDS:"

Love Never Ends
Gently it all began, so bewitching:
A thrilling touch circles my cheek, ignite
Racing hearts astir, hands clasp, we blushing.
And I lov'd you long before night drew light.

My love's desire utter bewilderment;
Kindles my senses gentle soft, breathless;
Ecstasy, oh, such love truly most sweet
Fires my soul, shrives all fantasy harmless.

Now ever am happy with memory
But more charming love's promise yet to come;
His mistress in all his thoughts, how lovely
Yet souls not of this world, Angels keep mum.

So, I from this place but never from you;
To watch my love, achieve long overdue.

Chapter Fifteen

Maria's Interest

Like a sponge, Maria continued to absorb everything; to be saturated with all the things I was doing and had to do with my life to date, wanting to know everything about me and my family, my mother and her background, her relatives, my sister. I told her all, all that I could in our short three and a half years over Skype. When Mother was first introduced to Maria, immediately, she liked her, and it wasn't long before Maria was part of our family; aware of everything I did, my family did in our daily life, my past, the present, the future, and my family connections with royalty and the aristocracy of my past. Her desire was to know more and more and everything possible of me as was I eager to know about her. Catching up, closing the gap of past separation until there was no individual past only one with each other.

We are great friends, talking every day now; again, lovers with such depth that few could understand or even remotely imagine. She wants to know everything that I'm planning for my future, demons or none. My Maria wants to know all, and she is always responsive either with good advice or intellectual commentary that helps to stimulate my deepest curiosities, focusing on the things that I want to do with my future plans, and many ideas that do not, and whatever, it always made for fascinating conversation.

Maria so wants me to come to America right now. When I explain the politics of the situation, she offers some ideas, writes then calls her congressman.

But nothing materializes. That Bulgaria is not yet a member of the United Nations is a good reason, politically. This is the year 2005. But that never holds us back; for the time, we enjoy and exchange conversation of our favorite hobby, photography, and continue to besiege one another with our favorite subjects: family and Nature and our love, and all the exciting ideas for me to pursue when I come to America.

One time Maria asked me if I ever think that what we were doing is silly and foolish, an impossible lover's game that could never materialize in this life.

"True, but, Maria, right now still it's not the most complete as all lovers know."

"You mean physically?"

"I do, my dear."

"Yes, I, too, again and again would love to consummate our love, Andrei."

"And do I remember us together sitting on the piano bench:

"I kissed you once, restful calamity.
Sweetest warmth, unmatched singularity
Heaven's twist so complete, it captivates
Total abandon, saturates reckless
Its promise: churning, agonizing bliss."

Smiling recall Maria continues my poetic beat.

"One kiss, all structure gone, how sweet is it."
Benumb'd, transfix'd, and now I believe that
Somewhere way before we were mystery.
Yet cannot sing our song so happily,
Till heartbeats match sweet echo's destiny."

"It's your turn, love," smiling back at me.

"Delicate lips press soft, touch exquisite;
Unwoven recall never be forgot.
Undone am I, lost, all senses silken;
Mystifying, luring, no illusion:

To hold your hand still storm-tossed emotion."

"Continue, my love."

"Yet, senses impress sweetest rarity
As we immerse each curiosity."

"Wow, are we good or are we good, Maria?"

"We are good, Andrei," smiling brilliantly across half the world, "and no distance between us. Did we just improvise a sonnet?"

"We did, my dear, we did."

"Did you record it?"

"No, it all happened too fast."

"Spontaneous improvisation, Andrei; I've done it so often on the piano. I will try to recall it in my quiet time tonight."

"On a given theme?"

"A kiss."

"Yes, a kiss. Is that what you think its title?"

"I do, my love."

"So be it; and a good title it is; simple and to the point. I like it: A KISS."

"All in iambic pentameter; imagine that: ABAB, CDCD, EFEF, GG and a rhyming couplet to end. I love your last four lines, Andrei."

"Thank you. It suggests so much yearning."

"Oh, Andrei, you take my breath away."

"That I never want to do, Maria, please."

"Understand, Andrei, I'm stating the way I feel; not only do those words take my breath away, making me feel helpless when talking about loving you, they bring me closer to you, imagining that I'm in your arms once more, sitting on the log at the edge of the forest talking, again feeling your warmth, feeling your heart beating next to mine; then walking to the bench overlooking Zakopane, my original hometown, my roots."

"The thought is romantic, Maria; but we are both equals. Whoever could ever guess half a world away and so in touch?"

And if we told anyone about this, they'd never believe us; more like thinking us two whacked crazies."

"Although we are living in another era, still, Maria, you are and always will be my queen."

*　　*　　*

"So, what is your latest outing, my lord?"

"To Pernik on horseback, tomorrow Boris III is to check progress on the new railroad and, on the way, stopping to visit his old friend: Great-Great-Grandfather Ilia on the farm. It's an easy trip on a good road; about fifteen miles from his state in Sofiya; his retinue will be with him, just a small group of his guardsmen, and before he gets to the construction site, Boris will have a little lunch with us."

"Oh, how I wish it were now, but now you must to work; I will call you tomorrow; I want to know more about your Great-Great-Grandfather Ilia and Boris III. Have a good day, I look forward to tomorrow. Goodnight, my love."

"Until tomorrow, sleep well, my dear."

*　　*　　*

"Boris would arrive about 9 A.M. and have coffee and a little sweet cake; it was more like a sweet roll-cake that my Great-Great-Grandmother Mara would make for him; that is, she told the kitchen pastry maker what was the King's favorite, and it was ready when he arrived. It's called Banitsa; a Bulgarian favorite."

"Can you describe it?"

"Dough rolled very thin."

"Thin as for a strudel?"

"Yes, yes. Well, wait a moment, and you can see it right here; Mother is making it right now; you can watch us in the kitchen." I was quite excited moving chairs about, so Maria could get a better view of things.

The computer was so arranged that Maria was always part of our breakfast. And we could all talk to her, and she would ask us questions and what our plans were for the day. It was unique; she was the fourth at our table; she loved it, and we did too. Every morning it was like having breakfast with my wife, my mother and sister Dora. It was fun; it was family altogether with Maria at the opposite end of the table to my right. And it so happened that this morning Mother, Fidanka, was making Banitsa. I told Maria that now she can see how it's done firsthand.

"And, of course you know my mother, Fidanka, chef par excellence. Mother, would you please continue: 'Okay, first I beat about five eggs separately, and roll them into about two pounds of dough; add one cup of yoghurt—not sugar; then ½ cup olive oil; ¼ cup of water; and ¼ cup of melted butter.'

"'Maria, it is always best for the yoghurt to sit in water for at least 48 hours, getting out the salt.' Mother was speaking directly to Maria; of course, it was in Bulgarian while I translated. It was a real international baking show. And Maria could see and hear everything.

"'Then roll out the dough, nice and thin. Cut into strips and sprinkle in the feta cheese and roll over the cheese into the dough. (Also, you may lightly sprinkle a little nutmeg on top of the feta; this will bounce out the flavor nicely.) Now smear butter around the bottom of the Pyres plate and place a rolled strip in the center of the plate. Then cut another, sprinkling in the feta, continue adding nutmeg if so desired, or a finely crushed pumpkin, and roll, placing one end next to the first and keep on wrapping it around, growing the circle from the middle of the dish. Continue with the next until the plates are full. Preheat the oven to 375 degrees; lower the heat to 300 and bake about twenty-five minutes.

"'To guarantee an original Bulgarian Banitsa taste, you must use either Bulgarian Feta cheese or Greek Feta. Greek Feta is also a very good substitute; either way the taste is Sofija Bulgarian. When taken out of the oven it is sprinkled with a little confectionary sugar, and it goes very well with good Turkish coffee.'"

"Stop! You're making me hungry."

"Am I?"

"Oh, yes, you know you are."

In translation everyone was laughing not because she was so hungry but her distance was half a world away. And that would be quite a reach for just a taste.

"But you can use the extra weight; you're so thin."

"It's this thing I have."

111

"Well, then come right over; I'll have it out of the oven in a jiffy and ready-hot on the table, waiting for your taste approval."

"Thank you for the offer. I'm quite relieved to know because I was just wondering how I was going to reach through the computer screen half a world away."

"Where there's will there's a way," and I found it so funny that I quickly translated to my mother and sister who also found it funny especially that Maria and I were so mentally synchronized (half a world away).

"It is quite funny, isn't it, and how I wish I were there right now. Just listening to your descriptive preparation of Banitsa sounds so enjoyable, especially your mother's demonstration, conversations and translations lends itself to an atmosphere of the best pleasant, good company. In the past as today the kitchen is still the center of all good household activity, giving important and influential people a chance to let down their hair to just be good people as they want to be, should be. Definitely, it was a more gracious and generous time, Andrei."

"You're right, it was. Earlier Mother was telling me that the dining room where Boris and Ilia ate was quite beautiful. A twelve-foot walnut table with burl wood legs and matching chairs. And beneath was a masterful Persian carpet; Mother said that her grandmother said it was massive, I presume it was quite large. The chandeliers and candleholders were all from Czechoslovakia; place settings were from Dresden and stemware, Swarovski, crystal, from Vienna. All this wrapped within the four walls of an oversized farm house, which also had three extra bedrooms for travelers. Remember it all came with the property the Turk gifted to Ilia; in return Ilia's sister, Vera, went with the Turk. That was no hardship on her part, for she and the Turk were in love, and their request was mutual.

"Politely, Boris would send a messenger, letting the family know what day and time he would arrive; thus, giving my family time to graciously prepare something special for him and rarely, not too often, a place for him to sleep the night. But whenever he came there was always a hubbub of excitement; though everyone in the household, including servants, took it all in graceful stride. To be quite frank, Boris III was never fussy or fancy; at heart he was a simple and kindly man who truly loved his people. Often it was my Great-Great-Grandmother Mara who served Boris coffee and Banitsa, his favorite pastry. Maria, this was all told to me by my mother, a true descendent of that last noble limelight."

"What a warm-hearted memory, and so well you relate it that I can envision it all."

*   *   *

"You also might like to know that it was my mother's great-grandmother's son, Krum, who was the business man on his father Ilia's farm. Krum acquired the contract to sell Singer sewing machines; he was an importer going from Germany to Yugoslavia, Romania, and Greece in the years 1918-1919. Before that all clothing was made by hand. Now, how is that for a step back in time through the Middle Ages and back, back to the beginning of weaving, developing crude dyes and making handsewn garments from pants, to capes, cloaks, ecclesiastical and aristocratic; from refined clothiers of France to present-day America and to the common man throughout the world. What a closed club: Tailors male and female were in big demand, especially those to the nobility. The Singer sewing machine, with exception of handstitched lapels and special graceful additions to woman's dresses and gowns, changed all that and changed forever the clothing world we live in; more specifically, the ingenious refinery of the company's technology was quite instrumental in providing delicate under water navigational technology for America's WWII submarines."

"That was German technology made in America, as my father would say, and still, it is the best, but back to Boris, Andrei. I want to know what he talked about, if that is at all possible to recall from conversations with your mother, Fidanka."

*   *   *

"Well, Mother doesn't recall everything and, as she says, over time memory fades, but the modern age kept coming, for us Bulgarians it was slow yet very persistent, bringing forth new technical changes, making labor simpler; however, Mother does recall that her great-grandmother said that Boris always wanted to discuss new production ideas and marveled at the efficiency of the farm; he always took great pride at the improvements in animal husbandry,

113

whether hogs or cattle, goats, chickens and most of all he enjoyed the developments of good grapes; after all that was the great complement to delicious dinners at banquets and festivals, harvest days and, of course, pious thanks on Holy Days. Boris always held the farm very dear, for he saw it a symbol: that its growth was connected to the growth of the country and its independence. An agrarian country self-supporting in terms of feeding itself was ready to make and welcome new improvements of technology and industry, education, small shops, business and the growth of a successful middle class, independent and creative; in short, gifts of a free people."

"That independence and creativity keeps on giving and reinventing itself. What you say makes sense, Andrei; that is what happens with good leadership in any country."

"And, Maria, America is the shining star, the example given to the world. I'm always amazed what your country has done in less than two hundred years, and now again it is exploding with new and creative ideas. Technically, it has given the world marvelous dreams and opportunities."

"I know. I'm so proud of its accomplishments; it's called teamwork. I recall a story of a South African gentleman named Henry Rough Wood. How's that for a nametag. I once met Mr. Wood at Mr. Maxsomovitch's house in Chicago. Seeing that his daughter, Dianne, and I were roommates at Beloit College, I was a frequent guest whenever the two of us returned to Chicago over the holidays or for an extended weekend; honestly, we freely frequented both our houses, always palling around together: the theatre, the opera, museums, libraries and concerts.

"Her dad and Mr. Wood were acquaintances from an earlier time. He was here in America studying different approaches to manufacturing, installing and maintaining drip systems for planted fields, agriculture.

"He told us that in South Africa there was only one university that was trying to comprehend the idea, whereas here in the United States, he had been already to over fifteen colleges and universities and each had more thoughts and ideas and operations in progress than he could have ever imagined before his arrival. He was stunned at such cooperation, interest and progress. Lastly, I remember him saying, 'It's no wonder as a country you are so far ahead of the world.'"

114

"I know, I know, Maria, that's why America is my goal.

"When I had the two doctors, Theresa and Lawrence, over to meet my mother, they were so concerned and understanding, and Doctor Theresa, as well as her husband, was so attentive and caring toward my sister, Dora, and her condition, that I was convinced that these Americans are some of the sincerest people in the world. Of course, I really wanted to go to America with you, but at the time, our lives were so different and so fixed that it was impossible; and I had a major obligation. When we returned home to our countries, everything turned unimaginable for each of us."

"Yes, my love, it did; I to my short but successful piano career . . . ."

"And who could believe that I to routine irregularity, just trying to survive."

"That is hard for me to imagine, but I believe I'm experiencing something now that is somewhat the same. But it's time for you to go to work; I enjoyed our conversation today. I'll see you tomorrow, my love."

"Until then, Maria, love you."

Chapter Sixteen

Revelation

The following day Maria finally told me that she had Primary Progressive MS (Multiple Sclerosis). I was shocked, dumbfounded. My first thoughts were how could this happen; how could someone gifted with such marvelous talent that comes along too rarely to a human being, especially in the field of classical piano; Maria who played and interpreted Chopin—one of the great heroes of Romanticism who made a new universe with his music, clearly fresh and original—an antithesis of sound and melody to the greats before him with its folk coloring and exotic harmonies; his was a new and vibrant music, exotic, subject to new laws, fascinating details to the last note. It seemed to me that Maria could read the master's thoughts, and revealed the delicate nuances of his soul through her interpretations as if she had an intimate bond with Frédéric, her first love, as she used to tell me. She, who is so deeply intense, irresistibly beautiful in spirit and soul is now forbidden to play.

"One day I noticed that my hands and fingers were losing their dexterity, getting tighter, stiffer; muscles in my legs felt funny, yet I could walk. I tried to cover, to make excuses and then returned to the wood shed where I practiced incessantly, but it was useless. The following week, doctors told me that my nerve ends were weakening; my arms, my body losing strength, losing control; my fingers their dexterity; never would I play the concert piano again. With that news, my short-time husband-agent saw his meal ticket vanish and divorced me."

117

*   *   *

Looking at her over Skype, I was speechless. Again, and again, my first thoughts were how could this happen; how could someone truly so gifted, blessed with such marvelous talent; particularly, one whose playing illuminates the heart of the Classical Romantic soul. For many listeners, private, personal, deeply moving, individually touching were her interpretations. I know because I was there by her side overwhelmed, carried away with what I heard. Already accomplished, yet so humble and unassuming, generous; so, sincere and understanding, possessed with such goodness in spirit and soul. I know; I heard it; I felt it. But never could I imagine her thoughts trying to rationalize her loss of such a profound, personal and poetic gift; such inimitable intimacy and why, what for? Why did this all happen to her? Clearly, her resiliency, her resourcefulness and determination were exceptional. And what an example; what virtue; truly, a remarkable woman!

With great independent practicality, Maria thought of her Biology degree, and made application to the National Park Service where she was hired. On the application was asked: What are your first, second and third preferences of National Parks to work in? Her first was to work in any of the parks in the Pacific Northwest. And so, granted Maria was first assigned to Glacier National Park as a short-trail tour guide: The Trail of the Cedars, Avalanche camp grounds, emphasis botany. The month was April 2000.

*   *   *

So, is there no music acceptable in all your infinity? Or are you refashioning her for a rap band? Oh, my God, what have You done to one of Your own magnificent creations? To see such light and then turn it out is one thing, for it is dead and buried, but she is so alive, so vibrant, so individual, and yet you chose to let her suffer this demeaning death. What's the matter, not getting enough love up there? So, what does it prove: that you are wonderful and she isn't? Let's be honest, the Great One screwed up. Admit it! For you did just that! To make things worse, you let slip to her Primary Progressive Multiple Sclerosis, the worse kind; it's deadly. Or do You blame it on one of the Four

118

Creative Forces: Perhaps she breathes too much Air; stands too close to the Fire; loves the Wind; or drinks too much Water? Which one is it? After all you're the Creator; it's not your mistake? Right.

No way could I reason her sickness except to love her more, for she told me pity was not on her agenda.

"It is for me only to see, Andrei, to confront in the dark, deep quiet night, sometimes not at all."

Andrei stuttered, holding back tears, when he tried to ask me again how it all happened; then he stepped back to reexamine his obtrusiveness, and withheld verbal explosion for his manifest confusion, although, without regard, his disdain for the powers of Heaven and Earth were quite vehement, specifically calling to Jesus. And I believe that my love does not know that he can never hurt the Creator, or His Son, the God of love, but in his desperation to comprehend, separates only himself from his goodness. Regardless, I love him for it, and I know that he's forgiven.

Chapter Seventeen

A Stunner

Doctors Lawrence and Theresa always visited me after hours and usually stayed into the wee hours of early morning before they left to do their early rounds. That was always a lift for me; I always felt so good sharing in their late evening early morning conversations. Sometimes the night nurse heard me talking and entered, asking if everything was okay; that she heard voices and was someone with me; she looked about the room and laughed at her intrusion, covering her embarrassment by asking if there was anything I needed or wanted. "No" was my usual answer. "But often I do talk to myself," I told her, "and stranger yet, I answer myself too." But I did ask the night nurse for just a glass of cold water. She returned, gave me the glass, tucked me in and closed the door gently behind her. Doctors Lawrence and Theresa stepped back toward my bed.

Whenever the night nurse came in, I always believed that the two doctors just slipped behind my bed curtain or stepped into the closet area or the tiny adjoining room. This was a natural occurrence for them, for they did not want anyone to know that they were that close to me, reasoning that some of the staff would think that they were shirking their night responsibilities. But I was always pleased when they returned from wherever they were hiding. However, there was one time I was truly surprised, wide-eyed, totally beside myself. But this revelation took some time because whenever the night nurse came in,

I always knew that the two doctors just slipped away.

This time they just faded into the dark, yet I thought nothing of it. When the nurse left, I saw Doctors Lawrence and Theresa reappear. Looking at my doctor friends, I was shocked, and I couldn't pinch myself for verification either dream or reality when I realized they were spirits now in human form. To prove it both came over to me and pinched my cheek. I don't know where or how, but I got the courage to ask, as they looked at one another smiling, turning to me: "Yes, we are, Elaine, and we have been with you for years."

"When playing the piano?"

"Definitely and before, way before that," smiled Dr. Theresa.

"How way before?"

"Before your conception," answered Dr. Lawrence.

So, unbelievable as it is, you, the reader, now know my little-big-spiritual secret.

"What about Andrei?" I couldn't resist asking because I had to know.

"Andrei," they smiled and chuckled in unison.

"Doctor Theresa said that Andrei has seen us more than once; that is, she hesitated, once together when we were doing silly positions, but that was to attract his attention so that he would always remember us."

"What were you doing?"

"Well, Lawrence and I were floating on our backs; then standing up walking around in a circle; then floating on our stomachs looking down at him and waving; lastly, laying atop of each other pretending that we were swimming."

"How old was he?"

"He was five years old nearing six," Theresa looked to Lawrence for confirmation who nodded his head yes. "I believe that young Andrei was dead for about a minute, or two?" Lawrence held up two fingers and Theresa continued her story.

"It was two minutes and then he was revived by the doctor. We knew that he was the perfect match for you, but Andrei will tell you more when the time is right, but I believe it had something to do with impressing his girlfriend."

"Right now, it's 4:30 A.M. And Lawrence and I need our coffee before we begin our rounds. Goodnight, sweet one."

"Goodnight; and thank you," smiling ear to ear, Maria was wide-eyed, ecstatic, and, if it be possible, more in love than ever.

*   *   *

The next day Maria was beyond containment, and she told Andrei that he must never lose focus; she was most determined.

"My love, you must promise me to never doubt yourself, for that is the culmination to loss. You may review and retrace, that is only reasonable. For you are the essence of energy; a vessel of human vitality, believing in yourself is the fire to accomplish, and America offers you opportunity and the freedom to do so. No longer will you live among usurping enemies, distorted minds of grubbing humanity; those moronic puppets who destroy human endeavor; it is through their narrow-minded stupidity, cruelty that divides worlds and destroys cultures; dehumanizes individual independence, crushing man's inalienable right to be free, to think to create. Seek knowledge for your own sake, my love, and how you justly apply it will give you power and your soul a grandeur all its own—a spirit that is unconquerable, truthful, and beautiful."

"I will always remember that, my dear; I will never forget it."

Maria was beside herself with excitement, joy of which I had never seen. Quick as was her exuberance, she changed the subject.

"Oh, Andrei, I love Strauss, his fabulous waltzes."

"I'm convinced there is nothing beautiful that you do not love, my dear."

"Same applies to you, my love. Isn't it wild that we have so much in common? Oh, Andrei, Andrei, you turn me on and on and on. I need you now; you know that I want you, and know so do you. It's just outstanding how we want and need the same things, and yet all impossible. But I know there's a way. I will think about it. So please help me."

"Any way I can, my dear. I am at your service."

"And now let us return to the waltz but in general the dance. This you will enjoy. My mother was telling me about a song that she heard once; it was considered the enemy of a good Christian; perhaps, as I recall, she was indirectly telling me to be wary of peer pressure dating habits. She believed that it was never good to follow the crowd, but to be your own self. I smile whenever I think of that talk, because for me I was always more concerned and in love with my music and Chopin. Really, my love, I never had any boyfriends

123

or hot dates as we usually all went to parties and dances as a group and then home. Did you have any of these problems?"

"Never any dating troubles; it was always easy for me to find a date to a dance; and some of the girls were loose while others were not, to the latter I was always drawn. In fact, it was with my dance troupe that I mostly hung with. Our common goal was to be the best, competing with one another and eventually becoming part of the troupe. It was a great opportunity to leave Bulgaria and see if all the stories told to us from those who returned were true."

"Were they?"

"Yes."

"You romantic."

"Yes, I am."

"One of many things I love about you."

"So, what was this song that your mother remembered that was so important to your education? I assume it had to do with sex education?"

"Indeed, it did and the song was Nat King Cole's song about getting your powder all over my vest. I cannot remember its official title. But the Catholic Church said that it was too provocative; too immoral, leading youth astray to making the wrong choices, getting emotionally too involved, leading to necking, petting, sex. Sex was a very exciting no-no word in the early 1960s; it was never to be mentioned; it was a hush-hush word, therefore, everyone quietly talked about it; whenever possible, everyone tried to get as much information about this special topic, and how it works and why it's so secretive."

"Quite unusual, but not so uncommon, for all our youthful curiosities are a jumble and need sorting."

"And did you go searching in the same manner?"

"Yes, we did, but we were boys, so we had access to photographs which were quite revealing in every detail."

"Sex was a bad word, never to be talked about except between mothers and daughters; fathers and sons."

"Same for us in Bulgaria, I'm sure."

"On and on it goes trying to control and prevent hyper teenage curiosities and all their exciting cohabitating activates; and it worked for a while then all was blown away with WOODSTOCK."

"WOODSTOCK? Oh, I've heard of that; wasn't it some big rock-'n-roll gathering somewhere in Pennsylvania?"

"On a 600-acre farm somewhere outside of New York City; it was a gathering, celebrating rock-'n-roll in August 1969 that got out of hand. I believe the gathering grew to over 400 thousand."

"Wow!"

"Wow, indeed, Andrei. A free and wild anything-goes party; a party of all parties with drugs, sex, uninhibited wild, loud music accompanied by horrendous rains. How's that for knocking down barriers, bringing together peace, love and sex."

"At the time, Maria, I was only six years old enjoying the peaceful surroundings of my environment."

"And I was seven, Andrei, enjoying the same."

"So, my dear, shall I hear more about your Johann Strauss, the Waltz King?"

"Indeed. Oh, let me think. Where was I, where was I?"

"I believe somewhere in Vienna."

"I'm always in Vienna, my love, and always with you."

"I'm happy to hear that, my dear, for I'm always there with you too, and we're dancing. And here comes Strauss into the hall to conduct one of his waltzes."

*   *   *

"How right you are, Andrei. Johann was writing and conducting his waltzes, while countries far away from Vienna frowned upon such subtle emotional music usurping stayed pretense, enticing all to loosen their moral austerity, giving joyful fulfillment to lusty feelings. It was a new bacchanal, a new calling; an emotional and physical communion, ravaging participants, come what may. Of course, that led to many future romantic engagements, secret assignations, breathless dalliances in dark empty rooms or around the corner in a secluded alcove, leading to leisurely or, in short, sexual 'quickies.' His music gave new delight to sexual intimacy."

"How so, may I ask?"

"Silly, it was all in three-quarter time. Nevertheless, encounters, daring and promising, of tantalizing, sexual imaginings, were to be continued with

125

the utmost delicacies; of the most subtle yet dynamic impulsivity; instigated with smiles, deportment, words and touches, inviting flirtatious nothings; all leading to everything delightful, all slowly beginning with the innocence of three-quarter time. Most of all, Andrei, you know there is no such thing as innocent three-quarter time, especially Strauss."

"And can you imagine their continued excitement, Maria, especially for him, when she removes her fancy gown, willingly removing uncomfortable undergarments of shielding linen, muslin or silk, slowly divulging ravaging sexual highlights, teasing to lay bare her lover's latent, pent-up carnal energy, baiting voluptuous desires of two passionate lovers? After such titillating intoxication what enjoyment follows?"

"He and she, married or not, participated, Andrei, whether one or the other did or did not, for all was affectation, shy and demure, proper above and beneath the table or around the corner; scarcely straight forward, never blunt. It was the style of the moment; anything goes and anything did with Strauss' waltzes; a flowing embellishment of all that is silken and fair in Viennese love and war. Simply, it was the era, quite delightful; it was open swapping that everyone knew but kept secret in the room, behind the door, on the dance floor; or smiling demurely to one another's favorite on display in the passing carriage on the promenade."

"Ha, ha, of course nothing like that is ever kept secret; but, Maria, what an era!"

"Yes, it was a wild era, and Strauss was popular."

"So popular that many times he was playing his waltzes in one ballroom then running to relieve a conductor to play in another dance hall, as everyone, who attended, wanted to see the Waltz King. Strenuous, but rewarding on too many levels to mention, I am sure; nevertheless, all had a wonderful time, affording new excitement for the weekend, heady gossip in between and newly planned assignations for the next.

"And Maria, how can such beautiful music conjure anything ignoble, especially encouraged with its refined movements of bodies embracing one another? Flirtations turns, graceful separations, leading back into the arms of your new love or revealing delights of an old love."

"THE ARABIAN NIGHTS, THE KAMA SUTRA was already published in England, thank you, to Sir Richard Francis Burton. That such informative love secrets were censored from the Viennese population, I think not; and if so censored, surely aristocratic dilatants of a more prurient nature all had surreptitiously acquired copies. Anyway, censored or not, such music leads to its own romantic cravings and creativity; subtle, tempting and endearing, always promising; whereas today it's more direct, in-your-face outright sexual energy, hit-'n-run animalism, like jungle bunnies hopping up and down all in the same room, infectious and communicable. Have a good day, my love; you're to work; I'm to sleep, if I can; after that rant, I know now I want you more than ever."

"And that's our continuous fever."

"Want to know more about me, Andrei?"

"Keep going."

"I've got you under my skin."

"I know! And I also know yours is soft, luxurious sin."

"Soft, luxurious sin; oh, Andrei, we're too far away for such tactile honesty, but I love it."

"It's tasty food for dreams, my dear."

"Oh, you turn me upside down; how would I look to you upside down, my love?"

"Delicious!"

"I'm in a spin, 'round and 'round beside me I want you, you; you give me a fever that is fire bound; I want you here for me for us both to go down; both to expound."

"The person within is the attraction, Maria; you are an uncommon breed, my dear. Your soul sleeps contented."

"Only when it sleeps with you, and right now contented is not in my vocabulary; for in my dreams, you and I are always there; bump for bump, grind for grind and always enjoying and practicing the art of the Kama Sutra in our Perfumed Garden."

"You are exquisite, rare gold."

"Have a good day, my love."

"Until tomorrow, goodnight, sleep tight, my dear. I love you."

Her talents, sensitivities, her knowledge, and more does Maria bring forth, especially the love that man's neglect has made dim.

Chapter Eighteen

Another Memorable Day

My interests were her interests, and Maria did all she could to influence me to look everywhere with my camera for the abundant opportunities that were waiting to be captured by my lens. So amazing was she with the knowledge gotten from her grandfather and his influence. That not only was she his student; she was his best student, the recipient of his knowledge that eventually was passed on orally to me, Andrei. More than inspiring were her intimate details of the great secrets of the past as daily she poured out her familiarity on the subject. Having no idea of what I was hearing, yet fully captivated by her carefully guarded details that overwhelmed me, providing great hope for America as I chomped at her intellectual bit; always encouraging and directing my questions with stimulating conversation that only a marvelous woman such as she could project.

* * *

"Truly, Maria, you are imagination's gift; its wild talent, exclusively, unobtrusive love. Oh, how I relish the fact that we have met again. Sadly, not in one another's arms, but we are once more together. Never can I fathom it, but I praise the gods as the Greeks would say, believing there is yet much more for us to come."

"Because, my love, we are one another's complementary angle; we are equal and the same, without which there cannot be an isosceles triangle; we are bound by three equal sides, you and I and our imaginations."

"But we are in different fields."

"Still one in the same, Andrei, for we are equal individuals with our imaginations animating the whole."

"A positive contribution to humanity."

"Indubitably, my love."

"Meaning?"

"Fully correct; unquestionable; certain."

"Really."

"I love you, Andrei."

"And I love my aria."

"That I will take."

* * *

Sometimes it was strange how we knew what the other wanted or what the other would choose; not uncommon for some people in love; then again, in our case quite unusual, or was it, for we were half a world away.

For instance, Maria sent me an album: THE THREE TENORS singing concert in Los Angeles in a baseball stadium, Dodger Stadium. I guess the trio had performed a few years earlier in Italy and were successful, even here in Sofiya I recall hearing of their success; of course, who could not like these guys. They were fabulous, and I thoroughly enjoyed the album, making me, once more, aware of Maria's diverse musical background. So, I thought this is what can happen when you have talent and live in America. Believe me, I was charged and wished I was there right now. Yet we were connected.

When we talked about the album, Maria suggested that we play a game; each was to choose one of the songs that felt most sentimental and romantically dear to us.

"What criterion should we use?" I asked.

"Let it be a melody that strains the emotions; a deep longing that never can be fulfilled," attractively, she smiled over Skype.

Next day when we met again, we carried on with our usual greeting and conversational routine. Then out of nowhere, as if she just remembered, she asked: What was my choice of song, the music, the singer? We both laughed as if this were a life-and-death answer when she reminded me that it was only a game, only a test of our emotional continuity. I suggested that together on the count of three, we each hold up our 3-by-5 card to see our musical guess: AMOR, VIDA DE MI VIDA, sung by Plácido Domingo.

I was shocked. She was excited, claiming that we are definitely on the right track. I told her that I didn't need a recorded song to tell me that.

"Tomorrow, let us try once more; if we miss it will still be really very good—a 500 batting average."

"What do you mean, Maria, 500 batting average?"

"This is a game, isn't it?"

"Yes, of course."

"Certainly, you've played baseball before or heard of the great American game; it's originally, better known, as the great American past time."

"But what do you mean 500 batting average?"

"Andrei, at the beginning of the baseball season if a batter gets one hit, he's batting a thousand; the second time he strikes out or grounds out or flies out he's batting 500, and so on."

"Oh, I get it," I quickly replied, "and this process continues throughout the season; when the season's over, his times at bat are divided into his hits: thus, his average."

"Correct. And it is tallied after every game and during the game."

"And this applies to us."

"So, my love, if each misses this time, we end the game; each still batting 500."

"Clever lady!"

"No one loses."

"I love you, Maria."

"That too is acceptable, my love, thank you. So, are you ready for one more at bat?" Grandly, she smiled back.

"Sure! Again, the criterion is?"

"Pick one song that really fits us both."

"There's a song like that?"

"Yes, my love. And you to work; while I try to sleep."

"Wait, wait, Maria, you're sure there's such a song?"

"Yes, my love; we are both subject to it."

"You know it then?"

"I do."

"That's not fair."

"Yes, my love, it's fair."

"How so?"

"Because it summarizes us, and it tells us something we both need to know. Until tomorrow and beyond, I love you."

Just like that she disconnected. All day I mused about her abrupt leaving. When I arrived home, again and again I listened to the album; then began to narrow the songs down and down until I was sure, I had the right one.

*   *   *

"Good evening, Maria."

"Good morning, Andrei, Fidanka, Dora. I'm having Banitsa for my dinner dessert. Apparently one of the cooks in the hospital is from Sofiya; imagine that for a touch of home."

"Mother is making Banitsa too. We have your place at the table, only we wish that you would dress more appropriately; still in your sleepwear makes us all want to go back to bed."

"Well, it's eight P.M. here and it's? ... I forget again."

"Six A.M. here, my dear."

"Okay, tomorrow, I will be more presentable, I promise."

"Maria, I'm kidding."

"So be it, Andrei. If I'm participating with your breakfast...at your table, as your wife, you are right."

And it was so. Maria remained dressed for morning breakfast; it made us all feel more like family and she really enjoyed it all. When Mother put a slice of Banitsa with powdered sugar on Maria's plate, she hungered like we all did, but she could not taste it. However, she had the recipe and often asked the hospital cook to make it, knowing a day ahead that we were having it the next morning. Now she could share in its delight while we had ours, all as family.

"So, Andrei, have you figured out the song that best describes us both?"

132

"Yes." Again, we counted to three; each held up his 3-by-5 card; I DID IT MY WAY.

"I knew that you would choose it because it's so like us. And we do so think alike, perhaps is telepathy."

"Call it whatever you like, it works. When I began to narrow the songs, Maria, immediately I was drawn to MY WAY; I DID IT MY WAY; it took a little thought when everything came crashing to me, for you and I are a rarity: We ask no favors; we ask no special gratification; we've made mistakes: bad marriages; great sacrifices for doing what we love; your piano, my dancing; your sickness not self-imposed; I in Bulgaria, isolated, also not self-imposed; alone yet we are dynamite together."

"Yes, my love, it's just as the song describes."

"It is our way, Maria, and when we get another chance it will be for us both, together, that's the best way. For now, it's goodnight, my darling, goodnight."

Kissing her fingers, she placed them to the screen touching mine; through her tears she proudly whispered: "So close in life, yet so far apart. Until tomorrow morning, my love; have a wonderful day, my love."

*   *   *

Quite often, throughout the day, at the most ridiculous times, I thought of what had passed between us. Our musical identification, definitely passionate; our individual determination; our sophistication; was it two minds from somewhere within our galaxy, or out beyond the stars that followed different paths then crossing as two parallel lines in space connecting here on Earth where instantly we fall in love, now traveling together helping one another; or is this another, once more, now farther apart, yet closer; so much closer emotionally, spiritually, loving. And so, we agree to let it rain; for as long as we're together, we can shed any storm; perhaps we'll learn how to walk between the drops, and miraculously she'll be cured; anything is possible, I thought, anything. Yet, this is not some romantic story that ends well or a film or even an opera where we may afterwards see its performers at a hidden or an exclusive, remote restaurant. This is real life with a real-live star who I love as never will I love again.

Chapter Nineteen

Happy Birthday

While at the store one day, I got a call from my banker saying that a check sent from America for twelve thousand dollars has been received into the bank, and I must come down to officially sign it into my account. "Oh, yes," he said, "there's a sealed envelope with your name on it."

A birthday card from Maria, I thought.

Take a vacation for yourself; have fun; do reckless things. I wish I were there to join you to give you many hugs and kisses for all the happiness you have given me. Happy birthday, my knight-my Love-Life of my life.

Love,

Your Aria.

The image of being myself, beside myself was absolutely clear; that is, there I stood looking back at me, that surprised, that excited. Maria and I had talked; she said that she wanted to do something for me for my November birthday, and she kept asking me what did I want. There were many things I did want, but no way was I going to tell her that; no, that's not right; that's not why I talk to her; that's not why I love her. So, the darling one told me, actually, commanded me, saying that this is her way, and I was to talk to myself, asking what did I need; what would I enjoy; what was it that the family needed; and what would they enjoy?

That afternoon I came home for lunch to discuss Maria's offer. Mother was very practical. So, I buried my pride, and the following morning, just before I left for the store, I told Maria what I believe she already knew: money.

"Very good, Andrei; this way you can do whatever you want; whatever is practical; for you are the best judge of your needs, not I. I am happy to help you and your mother and Dora, for, Andrei, I am yours; you and they are now my family. Now that is settled, you must to work, and I to sleep, my love."

I thanked her; then, as usual, kissing our fingers, extending them we kissed goodnight; reaching for the switch, I choked off tears when I saw my Aria leaning forward, beginning to whisper to me; her deep bight, faithful blue eyes were full of pride.

"My love, you've given me many beautiful memories. I close my eyes, and I always see you; your kisses are always with me, for no one has ever kissed me the way you have. And don't be afraid of wholesome tears, my love; they are a luxury, and you and your family deserve them. Have a prosperous day; I love you."

I nodded yes, turned away and was gone.

Chapter Twenty

Shared Joy

It was our second Christmas together. Maria and I were both very happy; she was just bubbly and so alive. Enjoying breakfast. She was our special honored guest, and we took great pride in displaying all the dizzying things that she and I, as she insisted, bought for our family. In turn, we took great pleasure is displaying the new clothing, dresses, shoes and pants and shirts for me and for Dora and Mother. But Mother's great pleasure was the beautiful light brown real leather purse with its adjustable shoulder and/or handle straps, brass buckles for secure closure. Not to bore Maria too much, but she persisted until once again I showed her the photos; that is, the top of my head as I lay on my back in the dentist chair while he worked on my teeth. Again, Maria said that it was wonderful to see me getting body together in preparation for my United States debut, which she was sure to come about in the coming year. She loved the new additions and renovations I had completed to the house: extending the kitchen out, more into the yard, adding the beautiful new thermal-pane windows. They were at least five feet high, about two and a third wide, making a very satisfying presentation, opening to the garden from the breakfast seating area.

I was very proud of what Andrei had done; I could see not only was he thorough but a planner, conscientious and careful with money, detecting also that he was governed by a sense of duty; frugal, not cheap, but a saver, another great quality in the man.

I loved the family photo he took of Mother, Fidanka, his sister, Dora, where he is slightly leaning over and between them.

My, my, how revealing. I could see physical strains of his ancient heritage: of modest height, barrel chest, a light swarthy complexion from centuries of genetic interaction; very much like the early Greek and Roman physics, now properly pigmented and varied from years of woven Italian genetics, dressed in contemporary attire; and how easy it was to envision that when they were all armed, locked together, arm-in-arm it was impossible to knock them over or break their ranks. With their shields over their backs, they became a road to the top of the walls to overrun.

Another favorite photo is of him sitting on a rock, looking out over his great-great-grandfather's inherited farming estate. That has to be my favorite. It's the back of his head that I find so interesting, meditating atop broad shoulders. It reminds me of an image I have of Belisarius, the noble Thracian, who was born in Sapareva, Banya southwest Bulgaria, not too far from Sofiya; married to Antonia, his wife, whom he loved and respected, but to her good friend Theodora, Justinian's wife, he kept a chivalrous relationship that each kept secret and aboveboard.

"That photo says so much about you: your wishes; your hopes, the plans called forth from a determined heritage, contemplating your strategy for success. I just love it. For you are my Belisarius, my knight loyal, my love and, except for my rotten form, you and I make a beautiful couple. Oh, my love, how I long to put my arms about you once more; then back to Vienna to love and waltz forever at Maxims or anywhere as long as we are together. Then return home to our pavilion where our sweet prize awaits us. Oh, my love, come to me, come to me, hurry! I haven't much time left, my love."

*   *   *

The following day, once more, Maria asks me to play a game with her, for she believes, knows, that we are telepathic. She asks me to think back to the THREE TENORS ALBUM and the very one song by which she will always remember me or I remember her.

"Oh, that's easy, my love. Furthermore, you want to prove that we're

138

telepathic, right? And you already know the answer."

"I do, my love."

My lady was quite excited, intently looking at me with constant deep blue eyes.

"I know you do," she whispered, visually locking me down. "And I know it's a number on the album."

"Oh, my, you are getting specific; am I to know that too?"

"Telepathically, yes; it requires specificity."

"The number is 15."

"You are in my head, my love, as you are in my heart, so tell me. From PHANTOM OF THE OPERA?"

"It's the only one I like, Maria: LOVE ME, THAT'S ALL I ASK OF YOU."

"Love me, Andrei."

"I do, Maria."

"And I love you so much."

"Are you surprised, my dear?"

"Never. For all the things we talked about, I did not want you to think me silly."

"You know, my dear, our love has been growing since our very first meeting and now with greater intensity as we enjoy each other's goodness. More so after you spoke to me telling me to ask myself what I needed; what my family needed. All that day at the store I began to put us, our minds, and our feelings together because of your request. How did you know, coming right into my mind, my thoughts and consoling me, my tears? How could you see them, we weren't that close to the screen or were we?"

"I just knew. I've been listening to you, I believe forever, but it only occurs when we are on Skype."

"The same is for me, my lady, and that's good enough. So just where is this kiss of ours to take place; I find Skype quite mundane."

"I too."

"And I believe we both know, Maria."

"In a quiet pavilion."

"Somewhere near the edge of a deep forest."

"Innsbruck, Austria."

"To end and begin our day."

(I have no body to give to him so broken and beyond repair, but I do have an active mind that we can both enjoy until next time, however soon that will be.

Chapter Twenty-One

Sweet Conversations Blending Intellectual

"Among the many things I love about you, Maria, is that you are not capricious, feeling one emotion then quickly turning to another. Oh, no, you are as constant as a breeze is fickle, coming from one direction then another either diminished or increased energy."

"Thank you for that! But Andrei, have you not yet figured out women?"

"What do you mean?"

"Women are eternal."

"Eternal what, may I ask?"

"Gods, silly boy; we are eternal gods; or should I say goddesses, it's less presumptuous; anyway no one can figure us out, for we are eternally charming, beautiful."

"To such truth, I will drink. And what a lovely thought it is. For I find you truly divine, intellectually diverse; a heavenly madness."

"So, my love, you think me mad; yet, I am constant in my madness, did you not just say?"

"Yes, yes, I did; whatever you say, but tell, how mad?"

"That every day I look for and take a new lover; as ready as the sun rises daily above the horizon, and I do this constantly as day follows day. And each day I wear out my lover, often many; by day's end, they're happy to leave for exhaustion's sake, just as the sun descends from his daily round to regenerate. Though unlike the sun my lovers never rise the next morning, knowing they can never satisfy the cravings for love that a goddess demands."

"Oh, my, I will reconsider my journey to America for want of stamina."

"But now that I have seen you, my love, I know that you are capable of magnificent endurance; persistence and delicacy beyond all measure. You are stalwart, demanding, yet noble, a refined lover, deserving of my love."

"You have such spirited ardor, Maria, that I am reassuring my courage to coming. No longer can I contain myself; you are truly beyond beautiful; I am coming."

"As in ROMEO AND JULIET?"

"Absolutely, I will come again and again, my dear."

"Goodnight, my love; you'll need your rest."

"Tomorrow and tomorrow, I will come again and once more again to put you to sleep, so momentarily you may escape."

"My champion."

"My goddess, sleep tight."

*　*　*

I had so much fun talking about goddesses last night that I simply have to let Andrei know how I really feel about the topic. And there are so many things that I want to tell him; to make him aware of the many opportunities in his fields of study that he might choose. Seeing that it is Sunday in Sofiya, we always made it a habit to talk longer than our morning usual.

"You know, Andrei, Grandfather always said that the gods and goddesses, who lived like ordinary people, were ordinary people but capable of substantial creativity; powers that we could never believe today and unforgivable tempers-rages. We would call them strange yet exciting people, a super people. For example, look at the Pleiades, closest star cluster to Earth, named by the Titan god Atlas, so his children would always know their home star; and not uncommon that other gods may have come from far away galaxies, far, far away."

"But, Maria, didn't you once tell me that you were captivated by your grandfather's esoteric knowledge of his heritage?"

"I did."

"I remember. His name was Sven, and he was a doctor of mathematics, taught at the University in Stockholm, Sweden, and quite a scholar in the origins of the gods."

"Which, by the way, he believed, my love, like I said, were real people who came from somewhere in the universe, some remote galaxy or from some nearby star—not yet discovered—hiding itself behind another star—to which some gods have returned... and there are many of these stars; gigantic in size, numerous; and yet we earthlings know so little of the world about us, before us, let alone the universe."

"How about an infinite universe, my dear?"

"Indeed, you're right."

"Very big on grudges, good example, Maria, is Poseidon, against Odysseus."

"And how's that for a genuine human quality, my love."

"That's big time, heavy duty indeed; often I wondered, what was their real-life human disagreement that has now become mythology?"

"No idea, but Grandfather always insisted that all was the result of we on Earth knowing and admiring them. Befriending them as part of the community when they were working with us; showing the people how to do things to sustain themselves, increasing their production; how to rotate fields, so to get greater yields, so necessary for our life to continue. Perhaps Odysseus was too independent, stubborn and may have insulted Poseidon behind his back; you know he was human."

"So, it is believable, Maria, most likely, then, these gods were large farmers, ranchers, with knowledge of the soil, animal husbandry; businessmen; ferry boat operators with shuttle services back and forth across the Mediterranean to North Africa, Carthage, Phoenicia; and out to visit Poseidon, brother of Zeus, living on Atlantis, now a great commercial and military power that was named after his son, Atlas, who lived there with his father and his nine brothers. Later, Poseidon and Amphitrite, his beautiful wife, had seven daughters, now located in the Constellation Taurus; put there by his brother Zeus, so his family will know from where they came, their home star. Nevertheless, six of these daughters are visible to the eye. The last daughter, Merope, is hiding, most likely behind another star, another sister."

"Andrei, who knows what business dealings Poseidon had with the European mainland and other towns and villages around the Mediterranean, even on the eastern shores of North America, Newfoundland, Nova Scotia and Maine where on some of the nearby islands off the coast are carvings in stone telling vessel captains to "Dock Here" for trading. It's all beautifully told through Oral Tradition by CRITIAS as recorded by Plato. Also, the man gods showed the people how to grow vegetables, grains, and it is well documented that both sides of the Mediterranean were growing grains long before 12,000 B.C. and earlier. As I said before, these people mingled with the humans, had extraordinary powers harnessed from within the universe that science today cannot even begin to imagine; can't figure it out, so, everything relates to myth. Yet only two thousand years ago we had another example of this power and human blending: Jesus."

"But our school's examination of these inhabitants, Maria, mostly comes from the Greeks and Phoenicians, who already recognized these legendary people as myth, some evolving from real human beings with extraordinary abilities. So, you think that these people lived thousands of years ago, long before today?"

"I do, Andrei, and it is found in Plato that CRITIAS tells his readers that Atlantis was existing earlier than 10,000 B.C., and I say much, much earlier; you know how myth evolves: from facts to legends; later legends growing creatively out of control into mythology."

"Yes, Maria, I follow that these facts grow, becoming legend, changing either by natural and/or flamboyant means until we have a grandiose finality—mythology, or, as you say, super people."

"Not unlike our Superman, the American science-fiction comic character, who came from the planet Krypton, located in another galaxy, to America and caught the imagination of the American youth. Superman is America's 20th-century man-god. And so, it was the Greek and his imagination's creative exaggeration, called metamorphosis, that grew these human-gods into mythological wonders, setting them atop Mt. Olympus."

"I've never heard of this Superman."

"You haven't, my love?"

"Well, you know where I live, Maria."

"Well, the America Superman fits right in with what we are talking about;

and not impossible. So, my love, stories about these special people grew and their involvement with humans came to be recorded by Homer, although thriving way before Homer. But why does it all nicely culminate with the Greeks, Andrei?"

"That's a good question, Maria; perhaps these stories were already here before the Greeks arrived or was it because the Greeks were more intellectually inclined, giving the world much literary and scientific refinement before its time. All those mythological images still have us recalling them in all their glory, reminiscing atop Olympus as a group of twelve or twelve families with all their bigotry, jealousy and erotic encounters—

just marvelous human examples of our contemporary daily lives throughout centuries before down to today."

"Grandpa Sven believed that the Greeks were occupying their country more than a thousand years before the Egyptians arrived, and they had a splendid education from the Naacal monks in India, the same Monks with whom Jesus spent his formative educational years. And you're correct, Andrei, legend grew them to live atop Olympus which is about 10,000 feet high. And I cannot help admitting that for gods they didn't rise too high."

"Bad pun, Maria."

"Yeah, but you laughed."

"That's because I'm into your esoterical side."

"Once more, my love, I insist that they were hiding among humans with god-like powers, looking for a good place to gather to picnic. Isn't that what we humans do?"

Again, we laughed at our own creative intellectual joke and then sobered.

"But, Andrei," Maria continued, "here is something to ponder. How ageless and forever beautiful is Venus Di Milo. What a magnificent sculpture is she, found by some shepherd in a cave or somewhere on the isle of Milos who sold her to some French curators who were searching the area at the time, or so are some of the many stories about her discovery. A good question: How long ago was she put into the cave? Who put her there? Who sculpted her? Whose house or villa neglected her? So, what happened? She is so beautiful; so precious, revealing the beauty of a society and its art. Have you seen her, Andrei?"

"No, but I know that she is in the Louvre."

"She's there; I saw her each time I played on tour in Paris. Some of the new scholars believe she was sculpted about 100 B.C., based on some marks they uncovered, which could have been added at a later time; of course, they have their papier-mache Ph.D. But no way do I believe these posthole diggers know what they are talking about or looking at, pompous pedagogic conjecture, nonentities trying to connect themselves with something greater than they could ever be."

"Her physical features and artistry, I believe, my dear, indicate that she was carved by Praxiteles from the earlier time of the 4th-century B.C., before the Hellenistic Era, which was started about 300 B.C. with Alexander the Great and his conquest of the Persian Empire, about 323 B.C."

"That's right, Andrei, and after his conquest, everyone wanted to be Greek. The Greek language was the language of intellectuals—a people who love to exchange ideas, looking for new ways, new approaches. And Praxiteles had such a beautiful hand in his work; so natural, so subtle, peaceful, quite human and then her smile, De Milo's smile, so warm, filling the quiet of the room with love, a beatific everlasting love; all a hundred years before Alexander."

"But, Maria, how does this tie in with Greek mythology; the gods didn't make anything, did they?"

"They were especially creative for who made up all the stories about the constellations and those enthroned in them; for good reasons or silly ones, like hiding someone or embarrassing someone. Or reminding them from where they came, and the stories around them remain infinite for the rest of humanity to ponder: Ursa Major; Ursa Minor; Orion, the Hunter and the Pleiades, he hunted; Cassiopeia the mother of Andromeda, just to name a few. These were humans who came to Earth from a star, somewhere, near or far, as a means of curiosity no less; played around; showed a few things to those they encountered then returned to their star."

"Whoever came before the gods?"

"You might say other sons and daughters of the Creator as a great cooperative human experiment; for are we not all children of the Creator? Jesus born of a woman, lived, showing us how to do things right; dies and went back home. Believe me, they were people, flesh and bone like you and me, but they had magnificent abilities; and you might stretch a few tales. But Andrei,

Mt. Olympus is only about 10,000 feet high. Not too formidable for Gods, especially when you compare them to Wagner's Valhalla and his truly imaginary, creative gods at war with each other, hating, cheating, sneaking and destroying. Reverse it, Andrei."

"What do you mean?"

"I put to you that they were not gods but human beings who liked to party on top for a family gathering or reunion—then again, maybe not; for sure these people-gods were here thousands and thousands of years before the time of Empires, MU, THE MOTHER LAND OF MAN, THE MAYANS, EGYPT, GREECE AND HOMER; then, again, perhaps it's all imaginative gibberish. Anyway, their antics, creative, imaginative or not, gave gossipy stories, fanciful tales of family's wild exploits; and why not? These people were wealthy, possible gaining it from working the land, businesses, and because they had money, they could do anything and get away with it. And notice later, these wild acts are not called hostilities or rapes per se. Just actions of spoiled people, successful people, wealthy people getting whatever they so desired— acting like gods as any rich man or lady today acts and is used to getting his/her own way—and because it was so long ago, stories became legendary, and more so after they died or returned home across the galaxy back to their star via some portal or some magnetic force. Remember our teachers have told us they were imaginary, mythological or whatever; and never any more. But we have taken the next logical step, my love."

"Maybe we do know, Maria, and it is also part of 'The Great Con of Man,' so we continue to let their legends grow, mysterious to the point that recall became more and more fanciful, imaginary, distant. And today to the learned, scholarly, or somewhat educated, it is referred to as mythology."

"Yes, my love, and not quite unlike the mysteries of the Holy Grail, or Jesus, stories 2000 years ago; born of woman, growing, instructing us by example how to live good lives and to be simply good humans. And there are his miracles. Because of human ignorance, jealously and greed, Jesus dies. He rises, walks about as living proof to all his followers and after 40 days ascends, returning to his father and his people. But he leaves how-to-do living examples, for his followers, believers. And His Church, in its original form, a very simple and beautiful religion: forgiveness and love."

"So, Maria, you're concluding."

"There never were gods roaming the Earth living atop Olympus or atop anywhere; but imaginative extensions. Planet Earth may have seen many people come and go; all kinds of people, perhaps for sure for hundreds and thousands of years. And the Titons were just another family dynasty; Cronos was Zeus' father. Like most teenagers Zeus disagreed with his dad, the ol' man. Zeus' friends—guys and girls—who also disliked that their family imposed a curfew and were strict with them—making them accountable—did something nasty about it, giving us good ageless examples of spoiled, snotty children with bad habits."

"Maria, your reasoning is fascinating; it's family, and how many times have we seen it throughout history and in our private lives within our own families."

"Disagreement in the family grew out of hand; violent arguing; impassioned, out of control; and his son, Zeus, and their younger relatives and friends beat up their parents, banished them to Titanicos, an old people's home, or annihilated them. No more brutal as were the later followers of Jesus' Church from Constantine in 325 A.D. throughout the following centuries with intermittent pauses for good Christian behavior. It's all typical human conduct, wanting to have our own way; children, parents, grandparents argue, fight, take sides, and become violent just to have their own way—to be in control, free of their human impediments, asserting their independence; in this case, and not unusual, over their families.

"That we see wherever we look throughout history, from peasants to Kings, in Shakespeare's plays, ROMEO AND JULIET, for one, Andrei, and today whenever people say they've had enough. On a grander scale, my love, take the American Revolution. That was massive insurrection against oppression in the form of taxation and no representation, no privacy, no decent court system or freedom of speech, or privacy. It was English colonial control. Then the great negation of the Native Americans where we conquered the country, more like just took away their land and homes because the conqueror writes the rules. I see you shaking your head, my love."

"Indeed, I agree; you are very correct, my dear, for I know firsthand how Communism conquered, stole, took away our peaceful land, and usurped my ancestral inheritance. The evil empire wrote their rules for lockdown political control; after about five years reluctantly some of the people accepted it, but they still, in private, yearned to be free. Slavery is not an inherent human right."

"Yes, Andrei, they were just real people, as reality ends in death or just disappears; after that fact, the tales, the legends grow, even about us today: Elvis Presley, Frank Sinatra, George Washington, Napoleon, Trotsky, Lenin; then those two idiots Rockefeller and Rothschild fathering numerous children throughout the world, believing they're gods while lavishing money to charities to make them look good, and the Russian Revolution could not have survived without their money.

"And that truly noble character: Chief Joseph of the Nez Percé who led his people to within 40 miles of the Canadian border. Here was a standoff between the worn-out, tired, starving Indians and the solders of General O.O. Howard. Realizing they were not across the border, his people starving, Chief Joseph surrendered. Beautifully sad his noble surrender speech is heroic and human. And what secrets of his tribe's origin we will never know. After a while—and that could be thousands of years from now—perhaps eons, his legend will grow and grow as will others—that is, if we don't annihilate ourselves first—slipping into mythology, grand and ridiculous, yet a beautiful contribution from the mind of man, as we know him today. Think of it, my love. Modern Mankind has been given wonderful examples throughout history and its poetic and philosophic literature of how to grow and mature his goodness to live a happy life, beginning with Plato's SYMNPOSIUM. All this intellectual and poetic, literate, and scientific fabric just does not develop overnight, Andrei. It's a collective whole of good and bad; how and how not to achieve presented and recorded for us to read, observe and do correctly. My love, Man is his family; his church; his community and education, education, education and all that is past. But if MANKIND does not nurture this, grow it, pass it on, he will gradually lose it, as I believe we are doing today."

"How so, Maria?"

"When money and greed become more important than honor and truthfulness is the first indication of loss of self, gradually a society and then a civilization."

"Your word 'gradually' is perfect, my dear; for all society will be lost; 'gradually,' it will slip away, and again we will return to our caves unsatisfied for lack of food and firewood and once more become savages."

"'When good teachers of literature and science and practical knowledge stop coming, education dissolves, society decays, and we disappear into darkness.' That's a direct quote from Grandfather Sven."

"You are on to something, my dear. Eons ago few people filled the world as we know it's abundantly populated today."

"As an exciting and challenging experiment in human cooperation, physical and mental and cultural blending; few brave ones did come, voluntarily, from other planets, a far or a nearby star, Andrei, if one can call a star nearby."

"It's poetic, my dear; or perhaps somewhere within our own Milky Way Galaxy, which, I believe, is 120,000 light years in length. Meaning that one has to travel 186,300 miles per second for 120,000 years to come to its outer limits; that is end-to-end."

"And its thickness is about 60,000 light years. Many of these people may be living deep within our own Milky Way Galaxy which is considered near compared to some distant place, Andrei. Maybe far into space, somewhere yet undiscovered, totally unknown; perhaps another galaxy—another infinity—passing right through ours."

"Totally poetic, my dear, and infinitely possible. For who are we to think that we always are first and know everything. That would certainly limit the Creator's imagination; yet, how ridiculous evolving from an amoeba or a snail out of the sea."

"That manmade concept is to keep us all off balance, guessing. If that were true, Andrei, we'd still be in our shells, sweating like hell, trying to divide somewhere on some remote, hot, dry, sandy beach."

"Or island, ha, ha." We both had a hardy laugh; two lovers enjoying their own smug, analytical conversation half a world away.

"Oh, Andrei, there is so much we humans do and do not know and refuse to know that it is sinful and can lead to our own annihilation."

"How true, more so when no one really cares, and I've tired you; it's time we quit, my dear; there will be another time."

"I know, my love, but, before we say goodnight, may we have one last poetic conversation?"

"All our conversations are poetic, my dear."

"True, nevertheless, you begin, my love."

A: Maria, is that you, my Maria

M: Yes, your lusty love from the Seraglio

A: Oh, I love this game of yours, my darling

M: That thou art my love, truly I obey

A: Wishful thinking but only for today

M: Least someone new correct my squirrelly ways

A: Absurd, my dear, you are my whirl, my daze

M: Tell me my favorite wind concerto

A: Oh, what a task, too easy to unmask

M: Now I see that you love this game of mine

A: Sly you are, now I must respond to thee

M: You do with such ease, marvelous aplomb

A: You think off guard, caught now I'm numb

M: Think that, so you believe, then I'm a nun

A: A nun, my lady, who is my mistress

M: Better yet that I am your temptress

A: My temptress truly thou art forever

M: You have delayed enough, answer clever

A: Mozart's C Major Woodwind Concerto

M: There's more, if you wish to see more of me

A: I do; so, hear play the Andantino

M: That piece reminds me of walking the path

M: To Heaven; the flute calls joyously plays

"Encourages me no hesitation;

"Pausing only to be once more sweet-talk'd

"Urg'd by its charming melody beckon

"To worlds seeing infinite all before

"Within the warmth of magnificent light

A: Magnificent it is, I will join you

M: I know you will; gladly I'll sit and wait.

A: Many friends you will make talking gaily

M: They will encourage me to keep spirits

A: For they know you have chosen to wait.

M: Joyful you linger on giving me hope

A: Count me no saint, just your loving mate.

M: I grow tired and need to rest, my love.

A: Late morning here and I've delightful thoughts.

M: Goodnight, my love

A: Love you, my dear

But tomorrow was Monday, so we postponed our fascination for more flamboyant out-of-the-box thinking. Once more, pressing kissed fingertips and palms to the screen—like holy palmers—then I to work about the house, she to sleep.

*　　*　　*

Once more it was another Sunday, and I so looked forward to extra time with my lady and our intelligent and fascinating conversation.

"Andrei, Grandfather Sven was a believer that the Swedish people came from somewhere in the South Pacific. Are you aware of MU, The Motherland of Man, located in the South Pacific?"

"You mentioned it briefly last week, but really, no. However, the articles I read on the internet did mention MU being The Motherland of Man just as you said."

"Yes, I did, but let me begin on a more tangible note, Andrei; my grand-father, Sven, had these books and some were first editions that he uncovered and cherished. Now I have them all, and I have instructed my lawyer, Wilbur Werner, in Cut Bank, Montana, to go into my house in East Glacier Park and forward them to you. He has all my information and wishes and the key to the house, which is to be sold or given to you. So, that is that and now back to our conversation."

"Maria, you don't have to."

"But you're coming to America, and I want you to have something to read, to be aware of America's many opportunities. Your photography is mar-velous, and you are interested in Photo documentation, as you have mentioned. These books then will give you more ideas, and our conversations now will help to generate even more interest for your future work. So, there! No more about it."

"Thank you, my dear one."

"You are more than welcome, Professor."

"Professor?"

"Yes. Someone with your mind, talent and curiosity will one day be a professor and a great teacher too."

"Once more, thank you, Maria, my love."

"And thank you, my love. Anyway, Grandfather Sven believed from reading these books that many races of people migrated across the Pacific Ocean from the three islands of MU, settling all over the world back into China, India, via the Indian Ocean and directly across the Atlantic into Africa, and the Mediterranean into North Africa and southern Europe. Remember millions of people were living on these three islands."

"So, what part of the Pacific were these islands located? So many people and nothing found?"

"Oh, much has been found and most likely by government, deliberately secreted away to continue *The Great Con of Man*. But are you ready for this; The Motherland of MU comprised of three islands; together it was a land mass larger than North America, which includes all Canada, the United States and Mexico together."

"Wow! My God, Maria, that's massive. Can we see it today?"

"Except for very few islands, no; because a great physical eruption occurred about 12,000 years ago, Andrei; volcanoes, earthquakes devastated everything in its wake, upheaving, sinking and burying anything, 64 million people were lost, according to documentation of the Masonic Order. Recall Pompey? Only this was larger and more explosive, unimaginable; the gas belts beneath the ocean floor of the Pacific erupted destruction, catastrophic is more like it. Paradise on Earth, it was: warm, abundant; the land quiet and calm laying in order with man walking and living upon it was now thrown up for grabs, dissolved, and disappeared with greater chaos than Pompey ever could be."

"Yes, I do recall Pompey, Maria, but nothing of your magnitude in the Pacific. And every now and then a scholar finds another area, uncovers more mosaic walls, and flooring, marveling at its artistry. But when I look at the map on the globe, which I bought last week, the Pacific is enormous and the island of that size can easily be located there for all to see... then, again, I'm in Communist Bulgaria; such interesting information is not easily available. One has to search for it—in the Black Market."

"And there is that marvelous Masonic BOOK OF THE DEAD, Andrei, writing throughout the years in commemoration of those 64 million people."

"I never heard of it."

"Forgiven, I'm sure it's not that popular in Bulgaria or even on the city's library index."

"I doubt our librarians even know of it. To me it's always exciting when something is uncovered and that includes being on a shelf too. Tell me more about this MU, The Motherland of Man. And you mentioned something about *The Great Con of Man*. I'm with you, my darling; it's all so fascinating."

"*The Great Con of Man*, Andrei, is nothing more than governments, powerful organizations and people in high and/or dark positions of secreted authority to withhold information from the general public. They want to keep the status quo of the curious few, the nosey, from disrupting the dull common day-to-day thinking of the masses; they want no challenging, no disturbing intellectual thought."

"I believe you, my darling; I believe you."

"They want things all under control: examples are too numerous to mention, but here's one: the Euphrates Valley, thought to be the Cradle of Civilization; or one better, Leakey's (1903-1972) African discovery which the natives showed him. You know that Louis Leakey's parents were English missionaries in Kenya?"

"Really?"

"Well, they were, and Louis was originally brought to the fossils discovered by the natives; he got excited kept nosing around and ended up graduating from Cambridge. The English Anthropological Society established, 1863, and the Ethnological society, London, 1843, was the first of its kind. I'm sure they both loved Leakey. His discovery gave them credence; later, the societies declared that Kenya was the first sight of fossilized man on Earth, but they forgot to tell us that this fossil was that of a man-looking ape, a hominoid-like a human, an animal resembling a human, and that we are to believe from this man evolved. Not that this discovery of Leakey's is irrelevant, but it's not of real human significance, although indicating a great deal of hominoid life on Earth one to two million years ago."

"I'm guessing, but I think that as we talk more about MU, The Motherland of Man, you will give me more pointers about *The Great Con of Man*."

"Right you are, my love. And why is it that our government has the Bermuda Triangle declared off limits?"

"I don't know, my dear, I'm still in Bulgaria, but I'm sure there is a good reason. How about hiding something; perhaps something related to Atlantis."

"Very good, my love, you are good."

"Thank you, Professor."

"And you'll find this interesting, Andrei. A few years ago, when Grandfather Sven was in Chicago visiting us, he showed me a postcard photo of the Nautilus. The caption read something like 'completed mapping the Pacific Ocean Floor.' On the back of the postcard in the upper-left-hand corner was the name of the Department of the Navy that conducted the mapping; and the name of the person in charge of the entire mapping operation was a lady. And I don't know her name, but I have it in my files back at the cabin in Montana. That will be one of the specific items my lawyer will gather to be sent to you; I'm sure that postcard is in one of the books; I will let him know so he doesn't become frustrated in looking for it. So, my love, you will have everything at your disposal. But I digress.

"So, Grandfather Sven called this department, expecting nothing but a runaround. And he was blown away when someone actually answered. Asking for the lady by her name on the back of the postcard, he was told he would be put right through. When connected, he asked if she was the lady whose name was on the back of the postcard. 'Yes,' she responded, 'and can I help you?' Grandpa Sven said he wanted to know 'if MU was still there, intact.' A total pause, stunning in its silence as if there were a blackout or disconnect. Once more, he said, 'Are you there?' 'Yes, I am' was her reply. Again, he asked: 'Is MU still there; is it intact?' She told him: 'You are the only person who ever asked me that question.' 'I'm not surprised,' he responded, 'I know quite a bit about it from books and Oral Traditional informants.' Totally taken aback, she quietly answered: 'It's all there, sitting quietly.' Grandfather Sven, also totally blown away, thanked her and hung up.

"Before MU totally erupted, Andrei, there was a good amount of warning time that passed. Volcanoes in the area were giving ominous signs, exploding setting off great fires, and remember these islands were large land masses, larger than Canada, America and Mexico together. Earlier, maybe hundreds or thousands of years earlier some people were scattered, exploring, looking

155

for other places to settle erecting identifying signs, like Stonehenge or the Sphinx to look for in specific areas for future settlements, for the islands were acting unstable for quite a while now, giving blatant warning to those living there to move on. And some already had. But when the gas belts exploded from under the ocean floor, crushing and rearranging everything in its path, it gave rise to the Rocky Mountains, about 12,000 years ago, the three islands sunk, leaving only remnants we see today in the Pacific, the massive statues on Easter Island being one. Hawaii also has some hidden remnants of that great island society. Already it was too late to leave, for leave taking was panic, loss. Earlier, before the catastrophe, others reached South America, Mexico and North America ahead of the immense volcanic activity, which since never has been repeated. That entire continent of MU disappeared. Some heeded those warnings like the trembling Earth, the shaking of the land, and the ominous volcanic activity, here and there, later today called the ring of fire, went ignored. (It is true today that the lineage of the Samoan people are directly related to their original survivors.) Yet, I cannot believe many remained complacent—for its terror was widespread and seen by everyone, at least by those who hung around. Over 64,000,000 died in the crush; many others got out anyway they could, and some were also saved with nature intervening to rescue fragile human life as recorded by the Native tribes along the Alaskan Coast. The stories, the legends are now mythological."

"But, Maria, people are the same today, not believing warnings, examples which were right before them; hence, many Jews who didn't want to believe Hitler and his evil, thinking he would be replaced and all go away."

"Good example, Andrei."

"Other things I remember reading about a Mexican serpent, Maria, but I cannot remember its name; it was something like Quat or Quet . . .?"

"Quetzalcoatl?"

"No, yes, yes. Wasn't it supposed to be a serpent god of the Mexicans?"

"No, no, not at all!"

"Really, I thought it was some kind of Mexican deity."

"That's what he has evolved into now or a little before our time. Here, again, mythology. Quetzalcoatl was a genuine man now believed by some to be a god. I might add that Grandfather Sven told me these facts that I'm about to tell you are not to be found in the ordinary history books."

156

"Maria, you're teasing me; I want to know!"

"When the Spanish gold explorer Cortez, because that what he really was besides brutish, ruthless and cruel, about 1519-1520. In his search, while in the Caribbean, he came to Alabama, where it was hot, humid and sweaty. Naturally, he encountered some of the natives in the area. Their chief was brought to him, immediately he believed that Cortez and his men were gods, after all the natives were impressed, never seeing humans with such splendid armor: steel helmets, breastplates, swords, crossbows, blusterous guns, better known as a harquebus; more so imposing were such magnificent beasts, horses; it was nothing they had ever seen before; they were amazed as were the natives Columbus encountered in 1492; actually, they believed he, Cortez, was the return of Quetzalcoatl, the ancient, mysterious god of the Mexicans; so the chief gave him whatever he wanted, but the natives had no gold. However, it is interesting that Cortez' scribe noted that the Chief was carried by four hefty naked men sitting on a carved wooden throne; also, the chief had on a cloak made completely of yellow canary feathers; according to the discoveries and translations of Churchward (1851-1936) on MU, the cloak was liken to the same cloak worn by the King of MU, thousands of years earlier. So, you see how these facts to legends to myths continue on while few remain unchanged."

"A real man yet thought to be a god, Maria."

"Yes, indeed, mythology in the New World right before our eyes. I tell you, Andrei, my love, it's all here, hidden and being hidden still. Again, when Cortez invaded Mexico and took over the country, he uncovered a library of the ancient Maya, three hundred thousand volumes. No one could read or decipher the writing it was that old, although it is said that some of the old families could decipher some words. I believe it was an excuse to avoid Christian interrogation, which was never pleasant. There were three or four volumes that Franciscan Father de Landa kept, and the library was burned. Later, when Father Landa returned to Spain, he was tried before a court of his piers for his inhumane treatment—atrocities of some of the natives—under the guidance of true Christian love. But he was acquitted, for he was acting in behalf of Christian judgment in his position as archbishop of the Catholic Diocese, of the Yucatan. Of course, Andrei, none of the natives appeared in their defense. Still, today, we are in the dark, or are we? And has this now become part of *The Great Con of Man*? For who were these distant Mayans? Where did they

157

come from? What great civilization were they a part of on MU?"

"The Spanish burned the library, completing the purge, and only three or four books were kept, hidden for sure. For how else does one get rid of the devil and his witchcraft? God burns them."

"But Andrei, total ignorance of perhaps a greater civilization; obviously, the Mayan people were from MU whose codes, ideas and spiritual beliefs and moral outlook of their society went up in smoke, why? Myopic stupidity?"

"They were not Christians, Maria, therefore without soul; no more than heathens heading straight to Hell, no big loss. Certainly not the type of leaders I want to be associated with. I know this is silly, but I would love to have met this Quetzalcoatl guy; a real hero and a leader, similar to Roland of Charlemagne's rear guard."

"And he led his followers, the Caucasian facet of the island, to safety. Already many had left; for example: The Black race backed into Eastern Africa via the Indian Ocean; others of the same race, closest to South America, sailed through the Amazon Sea into the Atlantic, crossing to Africa, and the Mayans sailing to the quiet of the Yucatan where family and friends were waiting; others through the South China Sea."

"But, Maria, what about the Rocky Mountains all along the Western Coast of South America? How did they get through?"

"Earlier, the Western mountains, the Rockies, had not yet risen. And many heeded the signs and left before the disaster, sailing through on the Amazon Sea, crossing the Atlantic Ocean to the Western shores of Africa. While the Blackfeet came directly over the Pacific, crossing what is now Washington, Oregon; walking East, they made their way to their homeland of today: All the lands east of Glacier Park, Montana and then some, actually, at the time, all was open for the taking. On the Western side of MU it was a hop over into China; or over the Indian Ocean to India where colonies already were established for thousands of years; and until four thousand years ago, it was the Naacal Monks of India who closely preserved the ancient teachings and religion of Mu. It was simple and what Jesus taught: love and forgiveness. So for Malaysia, Cambodia and Thailand whose jungles today reveal astonishing structures of stone constructed eons ago accompanied with marvelous sculptures of gods of wisdom and love. It was and still is a very intricate societal development much of it abandoned due to the jungle growth of years; now filled

158

with more mystery, which naturally helps to keep *The Great Con of Man* intact. Yet there are the Samoans who before all this destruction were sailing to their new settlements in New Zealand, Australia, just as we find them today; so, Andrei, the Samoans are still connected to The Motherland of Man."

"And yet, not all revealed to the world."

"Don't forget, Andrei, it was unprecedented mass destruction, yet The Motherland was spreading it culture or cultures via its displaced citizens whether or not people believe it today. For example, and still concealed today, the Egyptians were first Mayans, evolving from Middle America before and after the devastation of MU."

"And, Maria, we all seem to forget that we are talking thousands of years; it is all very possible, for humanity is curious, terrible inquisitive and very creative; as you said early man may have had powers that are today inconceivable—connecting with the spirit world, magnetic forces, gravity and beyond."

"Oh, I love you, my dear, because you are so right. And these early pioneers made their way to the deserts of Arabia while others nosing around walked and sailed right into the Mediterranean Sea, establishing visible signs perhaps thousands of years earlier telling those coming after that they were in the right place, Stonehenge, the Pyramids, the Sphinx.

"Centuries later it was Churchward, you know, who deciphered some, if not all, of these carved stone images, thought to be evil, an assumption of Father de Landa, the Franciscan, and found many of them relating to a very early and complex society; a people with great outlook and wonderful powers and machinery that we today have never witnessed.

"Le Plongeon (1826-1903) and his wife, Alice Dixon (1851-1910), about 1873, photographed together and documented much of the area of the Maya Yucatan. Both were shunned by university and clerical authorities. Why? Not only did they think them cuckoo, but their revelation raised too many questions as to who we are and where we came from, as thought from Asia. Not at all, Andrei; the Mayans came from MU and were totally decimated in the volcanic uprising, but, with many stops and starts, they continued the civilization that we know today, albeit watered down. Oh, how all fascinating it is, my love.

"You know, Andrei, when Solon, the Athenian Lawgiver, traveled to Egypt upon his retirement about 600 B.C.; he met with some of the scholarly Coptic priest of the Temple on Sais, one of the fertile islands on the delta.

Solon was to retire and informed them that he was determined to write a history of the Greeks and their relations with the Egyptians. Well, the Coptic Priests were so pleased, they began to tell Solon about the invasion of the Brazilians and later the Argentines who came from the Western world to conquer Egypt, and it was the bravery of the Greeks, who beat them away. They told how the Greeks defeated the Brazilians and later with the Argentineans. The Greeks had Argentines surrounded and were ready to conclude a massacre when the Greek leaders gave the Argentines an option: 'We will let you live if you lay down your arms, get on your boats, return home, never come back.'

"In a matter of hours, the Western warriors were gone. And later, again, it was the Greeks who so bravely beat back those from Atlantis; a few years later an earthquake demolished Atlantis, military problem solved. Of course, few then and fewer today believe in the existence of Atlantis; all fairytale, apocryphal according to some, but not those openminded readers of Plato; but it is real, legendary, and now the powers that be insist that it is myth—just another *Con of Man*.

"Then once more we have documented by that on-again-off-again Christian, Seneca. At the end of Act II of his MEDEA, where he has the chorus talk about Oceanus blocking the way to the great new land in the West America—which was already know to the Atlanteans 12 thousand years earlier. Andrei. It's all simply marvelous, my love!"

"Another curious question, Maria, perhaps also deeply hidden in the Vatican library is Columbus' first journals sent by Isabella to Rome. How much of this did Columbus known from his younger days on the sea, and how much more did he really discover? He was an Italian; and was open to the literary sailing tidbits passed on by sailors. Young and eager his ears were open, susceptible."

"Of course, Andrei, I believe there are more documents verifying all this, but they are deeply hidden by some government under some secret pact which includes to the government an annual financial numeration for keeping them secret, continuing *The Great Con of Man*.

"Same is true, my love, of Machu Picchu, the little community almost 8000 feet high in the Amazonian jungle; most likely it was near sea level at one time and rose to that height via the rising of the Rockies, 12,000 years ago. And so many building rocks set and interlocked so perfectly. Later I will tell you how this was accomplished, and to this day geologists say that the entire area is still subject to earthquakes."

"Yes, Maria, just as was Mexico City, for it too was at one time at sea level and now 7400 feet. Places like Egypt with its Sphinx, and its pyramids are quite old then."

"More than 100,000 years old, my love; archeologists will confirm 80,000; some of the more imaginative ones 100,000 years, but the pyramids were already knows as signs of a safe place from devastating earthquakes; furthermore, some of those pyramids point to particular stars and constellations, indicating perhaps some of man's origins. And I do believe that the pyramids of Middle America, Uxmal, Palenque, Chichen Itza not only were built to search for their own star high above in the clear night, but also to gather and harness some of the powers of the surrounding universe besides being a beautiful playground for favored girlfriends of the High Priests of the time."

"It all fits, Maria, for we are human beings, clever and intent on survival."

"Indeed, my love, and the search continued for other habitable places, declared safer than the islands. Stonehenge and much of the land in its surrounding area was considered safe for habitation and the continent of Europe; not to forget Finland, Sweden, Norway, cold but safe for Quetzalcoatl's inhabitants; India and Africa were large, deep and unexplored; nevertheless, safe, and smart people were leaving. They were slowly migrating all over the world into caves, and other safe shelters in Australia, New Zealand. Many of the Native Americans came direct via the Pacific Ocean; later, after the Rockies rise, the Bering Straits, developing the Old North Trail for others to follow on down into the continent of Americas ten, fifteen, twenty thousand years ago and earlier; proof is all over and out a little way from the Old North Trail. And before that time, there are Navajo tales of Coyote emerging from the waters telling the Navajo that another rebirth is to follow, I believe it was the fourth rebirth, as I imagine their home star, the islands of MU then to Middle America and finally emerging in Southwest, Arizona. Andrei, the original inhabitants of MU were spread throughout the world and meeting other people from other places.

"Then, my love, there is Triquet Island midway up and just off the coast of British Columbia; it is recorded—a proven fact—to have existed twenty thousand years ago. Revealed by a woman, a student archeologist at the

161

university of British Columbia. None of her professors believed her until she produced tangible proof.

"Another time, Andrei, I remember reading in a Phoenix newspaper about some camps that were uncovered in Alberta, east of Edmonton, 12,000 years old; the other east of Calgary was 11,500 years. Even earlier, before the Pacific islands broke up, people came straight into parts of South America, to establish workable colonies, Uxmal, Chichen Itza as I mentioned earlier, and so many more that were constructed way before MU's demise and now covered over for thousands of years with new structures of natural moist jungle growth. And then those marvelous individuals—the Cliff Dwellers—who traveled up the rivers to settle in the high caves of Arizona, Utah, New Mexico long before Mu collapsed. Too much to find; yet it's all there, symbols and codes, directions on the walls, but people are too lazy to put it to order. So, easily continues *The Great Con of Man.*

"Stonehenge, Andrei, was considered another safe place to settle, and the English—integrated by the Saxons—are still there today, and in earlier days were greatly admired by Caesar until Claudius outmaneuvered them in 43 A.D.

"Centuries later it was Churchward, you know, who deciphered some, if not all, of David Nivens' (1850-1937) carved stone images, thought to be evil, an assumption of Father de Landa, the Franciscan, and found many of them relating to a very early and complex society; a people with great outlook and wonderful powers and machinery that we today have never witnessed.

"Le Plongeon and his wife, Alice Dixon, marvelous people and intrepid explorers. In 1873, together they photographed and documented much of the area of the Maya Yucatan. Both were shunned by university and clerical authorities. Why? Not only did they think them cuckoo, but their revelation raised too many questions as to who we are and where we came from, as all thought from Asia. Not at all, Andrei; the Mayans came from MU and were totally decimated in the volcanic uprising, but, with many stops and starts, they continued the civilization that we know today, albeit watered down. Oh, how all fascinating it is, my love."

"Maria, what about David Nivens? I remember reading on the internet that said he was a mineralogist."

"True, of par excellence, Andrei, whose work in discovering buried Mexican cities that were possibly way before those of Mitla, Palenque and Chichen

Itza, but he was pushed to the side; beside so much more, he even found a jade carving of a tiny Chinaman; and this form of jade was nowhere to be found in Mexico, but in China; he concluded trade between these two lands. I know that's a stretch, Andrei—a particular to a general conclusion—but I'm sure more such artifacts have been found, and confiscated—keeping *The Great Con of Man* intact, the powers that be in control while laughing at Nivens' assumptive conclusion. Even today many Chinese have businesses and families that have lengthy histories in the area of Mexico that would prove an interesting ethnographic study."

"Maria, I also read that Nivens confirmed that Mexico City, at one time was at sea level, but rocks, soils, and sand, once at sea level, were now at 7400' above sea level; and now Machu Picchu, Peru 8000' above sea level; just incredible the rise of the youthful and powerful Rocky Mountains, calculated about 12,000 years ago. After all their peaks have not even begun to wear down as are the Appalachian Mountains."

"How true, Andrei; and how true is that the soil atop the Rocky Mountains is millions, hundreds of millions of years old, so are the mountains that old? Not at all; that's just dirt on the ground or deep within the top soil that is exposed by abrupt mountainous emergence, elevation. The Rockies Mountains are youngsters, Andrei.

"Remember that Nivens' work on the buried cities of Mexico uncovered some cities as far back as the recent Pleistocene era (early man 1,000,000 years ago) and others back to the Tertiary era (much more than 1,000,000 years ago). While digging in one of these older cities, he uncovered a carved stone pictographic.

"When having lunch one day at an outdoor nondescript establishment with Churchward, the stone was on the table and the two men were discussing details and interpretations. A boy about twelve came by and was fascinated with the stone and told the two men that he knew where there were many more such stones. Nivens offered the young man a dollar if he would get more such tablets. The young man did them one better saying that he would lead them to where he knew there was more scattered about and piled in a cave. Thus, Nivens uncovered about 2600 carved stone pictograph tablets; all similar to the ones years earlier showed to Churchward in the secret underground library in India by his friend the Rishi. And I believe there is one more set of

2600 that was uncovered. But get this, Andrei; the jealous authorities said that he, Nivens, carved these stones to insure his own notoriety. What morons."

"But Maria."

"Yes, my love."

"There's nothing humanly new here, my dear, not even today, because there are morons everywhere. They're guaranteed forever."

"So true, my love, so true," and we had a good laugh. "But everything was considered unimportant, and Nivens was labeled a crank by envious arm-chair archeologists. At the time, those in power framed him by declaring that he had no degree in the field worthy of such exploration or such conclusions; his imagination and curiosity, keys to great or just simple exploration, was laughed at. He was a well-educated mineralogist, and not afraid to get his hands dirty. Oh, I mustn't forget jealousy; it's as simple as all that, Andrei."

"And Maria, how few to none really know about the oldest library in China; it's located in Ningbo; and it, probably, may have some of the oldest documents, manuscripts of MU, and no one pays it any attention. Of course, it would be helpful to know ancient Chinese, as it would be to know ancient Coptic Egyptian for the stories that were told to Solon by the Egyptian High Priests."

"Marvelous, my love; you've done some homework. But I do not doubt these works have been translated and are kept in deep seclusion, quietly con-tinuing *The Great Con of Man*. The creation of the world, Andrei, has always fascinated man, just as some of its inhabitants."

"Man's origins are ancient, Maria; what a fabulous topic. If only I could photographically document some of it, wow!"

"You will, my love."

"I can hardly wait, my dear."

"My Grandpa Sven really was on the right track."

"Indeed, he was. And I find it quite fascinating that Quetzalcoatl was a man. What else about him did your grandfather find?"

"Well, before the breakup of MU, Quetzalcoatl led his people to Colum-bia. Had conflict with some of the pigmies in the area; made an agreement to stay long enough to build boats; and within six months set sail, once again, to settle in Norway, Sweden, and Finland to live in peace. Despite our modern-day conflicts, WWII, Grandpa Sven also figured out that to maintain their peace, the Swedish government remained neutral for the world to see, but, clandestinely, acted as a banking center for the Nazis, funneling money to Argentina. Thus, the Swedish continued to practice political delicacy, learning from the example of Quetzalcoatl when dealing with the Pigmies in Columbia."

"Quetzalcoatl was quite a resourceful leader. And Maria, leaders in those days were at the front of activity. Did he stop over in Atlantis?"

"I believe Atlantis was long gone, sunk by earlier upheavals in the Atlantic, and some artifacts can be found in the museums along the coast of northwest Africa; the coast northwest of England, Wales, Ireland, and down in the Bermuda Triangle. And I recall seeing on television a documentary of two sea divers who filmed and entire plaza floor and some columns still erect at the bottom of the Bermuda Triangle, and I never saw it again. This knowledge is very old and mostly now still recalled by Oral Tradition.

"Natives in the Dakotas, North and South, claim to be from Atlantis, particularly the Sioux. With my work in the National Park system, I have met a few who have told me so, particularly when I worked in Glacier Park, Montana. It was there that I met a man who was Sioux and working with the Blackfeet Tribe studying water rights. His name was Clyde Waln and he had heard me play when he was in Washington, D.C.; we had a delightful conversation at his office in Browning, Montana. He invited me to a dinner party presented by his wife Louisa Waln and Martha Kennerly, wife of the Blackfeet gentleman, JR Kennerly, better known as JR, who was working with Clyde. All was very relaxed; and it was at this time, during dinner, that Clyde told me that the early Sioux were from Atlantis, the famous island now sunk in the Atlantic Ocean. And Atlantians knew of America, the land to the West. One way or another, trade is money, my love. And perhaps a good reason for the hostilities to Louis and Clark's expedition up and their return down the Missouri.

"Later when I gave it some thought, I concluded that his story was not hard to believe, for his skin was light as were his wife and children who also had blond hair and blue eyes."

"This entire cultural and racial thing, Maria, is really quite exciting and growing today, as I am sure it did before."

"But get this, Andrei, Poseidon settled in Atlantis; had ten sons and they too had a big family. Sooner or later, these restless people from Atlantis conquered parts of Africa, Egypt and Asia Minor and Europe until the Athenians stopped them, as I said earlier. And these people of Atlantis were quite familiar with America. (It is also recorded in Seneca's play, MEDEA, where the chorus, at the end of Act II, tells of a new land to the West that will one day be discovered when Oceanus, the god of the sea, releases his grip and the great sea is once more made passable for man to discover the lands to the West.)"

"Then again, Maria, the entire world was not as we know it today. And the great land across the sea to the West was already legend and growing toward mythology; furthermore, if the gods were real gods, they could have stabilized calamitous situations, and all would be smooth sailing, don't you think?"

"That's my whole point, my love. These were all real people, Andrei. For who knew how to harness the powers, the vibrations of the universe. You might even say that they were connected with the Angels above or a superior force that overlooks all of us here on Earth. And you might speculate that, at one time, Earth was part of Heaven. Land masses all connected, pathways known. Thus we have man and his animals descending; land breathing, separating; eventually, we, have today."

"Good thoughts, Maria, interesting, very interesting, my dear."

"Again, my love, we have a dramatic awareness in Sophocles' play ANTIGONE. Antigone is condemned to death for defying her Uncle Creon's order not to bury her brother, Eteocles; however, before she goes to her death, she tells Creon, the new King of Thebes, in a heated argument that he, too, and all his phony gods will one day have to answer to the Creator, the only one before all, above all, who created us all.

"Yes, Andrei, translate the Greek alphabet and think about what it says. No doubt about it, the Greeks knew of MU, The Motherland of Man, and that there was one great Creator. Like people today there were also those who believed; those who did not believe: skeptics, atheist or whatever, they are everywhere. And, Andrei, most of the Greek legends, now myths, are similar and in all cultures with their particular culture's twist and location. Few present-day cultures have continued to maintain some of their legends. Nowadays these myths are only challenged by few, if any; and if anyone believes in these myths today, they would be discredited for being foolish, ignorant, and uneducated, but they nonchalantly accept them as sure as breakfast is served with coffee or tea."

"Agree, but what do you mean foolish, Maria?"

"Oh, I'm getting tired."

"Then let's quit; you need your rest."

"No, no, I'm fine, my love. You see, it's an old trick, Andrei, to discredit those thinkers who are way ahead of their colleagues. This type of person is irritating and annoying to those in charge, most of the time making one look ignorant or stupid. So, in today's world you can't burn them, but you slander them to get rid of them, shut them up. Set them up as crazy, cracked pots, deranged; or perverts by planting pedophilia, photos in their house or desks at work, not uncommon in highly sensitive government work, particularly if those in charge, find you an irritant, a whistle blower, a tattletale, a do-gooder who wants to see honesty, truth prevail. All is part of the underhanded *Great Con of Man*, to discredit one or someone, or a group—simply to keep control.

"For instance, Dr. Leakey (1903-1972), whose parents were missionaries in Kenya, finds a fossil—most likely brought to him by his buddies—of ape's human evolution on Earth, confirmed to originate in Africa. So, these apes could stand on two feet similar to man: hence the evolution of man via apes and Africa his origin. Even though you and I find this absurd, it shows the curiosity of man wanting to know his origins on Earth. After all, the greatest reassurance is knowledge and how you use that knowledge; so, the quest continues in earnest."

"But, Maria, my dog can stand on his two feet and walk a little, therefore he's part man. I find this reasoning hilarious."

"Absolutely, Andrei, but the search was on, and no way was anyone interested in MU, The Motherland of Man. That there could be another place of man's development on Earth was unheard of, nonsense, delusional, as witnessed by the burning of 300,000 volumes by Father De Landa. Anyway, schools, textbooks, some Bible studies build their curriculum about Leakey's discovery of early humanoids. No one individual or any one society was going to promote a new angle and rewrite the books about early man, ridiculous. By those is power, it was concluded a done deal. So how's that for an in-your-face *con of man*. Years earlier women thinking was unheard of, particularly suggesting religious thoughts or ideas; if so, sound familiar? She was simply condemned, a witch, a devil; banished burned or drowned, for that's how you eliminate a devil, the competition—sound familiar?"

"Oh, yes, even today, Maria, in my country, you dare not speak out your ideas or disagreements or impose too many suggestions; it's very dangerous."

"Not unlike examples, Andrei, of the crazies in churches or little townships in early Northeastern America, where an enfeebled woman was sick; or she stuttered; had palsy, a paralysis accompanied by involuntary tremors; she slurred her speech, or the fingers on her hands were gnarly, arthritic. She may, could be, and in most instances was considered to be a witch and burned at the stake, again familiar, compared to drowning of the early thinking Christian women.

"And. My love, you will find this interesting. All revelations mystifying or scholarly are to be checked held at bay; concealed and locked away by orders of the powers that be in these organizations. A few of those who made some remarkable discoveries were told to cover up or lose their prominence as scholars in the present or have no future in education and would be blackballed.

"Le Plongeon and his scholarly wife, Alice Dixon, were first to document in the 1860s, via photography, the pyramids and some of the hidden secrets of this middle America society. Yet, they were shunned, not even half their work published. They were blackballed, laughed at, rebuffed by their colleagues of intellectual society.

"James Churchward, the inquisitive tea broker from England. When in India, he made a new acquaintance who introduced him to marvelous discoveries and led him to explore underground libraries of deep hidden secrets— volumes of Man's early life and his work way before our time. Yet all this curiosity and scholarly revelation was considered bogus, quashed.

"There was William Nivens and his work on Mexico City from sea level to eight thousand feet.

"Finally, my love, but hardly last, was Margaret Mead (1901-1978), who uncovered much by listening to the Oral Traditional stories of the native Samoans, still living in the Pacific, who related stories of their ancestors living there on MU, thousands of years earlier. Word got around and soon she was visited by the Jewish League and Catholic representatives—each protecting his true faith. They flew out to talk to her—to scare her into abandoning her work in the Samoan Islands where she encountered glorious structures, temples: one hundred to three hundred feet long; twenty to fifty feet wide still standing on some of their five-foot-thick walls still intact. The religious congregation told her 'that mankind was not ready for such revelation.' By forfeiting her journals, Margaret Mead was rewarded with a prosperous life as a respected anthropologist, by keeping her secrets and contributing to *The Great Con of Man!*"

"Well, my dear, your grandfather was certainly sharp in his thinking, just as you indicated. And through you his ideas are fascinating, probing; I'm getting quite an education; it's good material to think about. Not only is he intelligent, he's curious, and that makes him a first-rate guy in my book."

"Definitely, Grandpa Sven was an individual thinker, a good scholar, and, yes, he was very curious. Forgive me, my love; I'm exhausted; can we continue another time?"

"Of course; to bed, my dear one, to bed; we'll talk again. Forgive me."

"I have much to say, and too little time left to make you aware of the many opportunities in America and elsewhere for you to probe and document, if you wish."

"Quiet, talk no more, my dear one."

"Goodnight, my love."

"Goodnight, my Princess, my Professor."

Once more kissed fingertips pressed to the screen as palmers say goodbye.

*   *   *

Another open Sunday and once more the lovely one and I carried on another fascinating conversation, making me aware of many roads to look down when I come to America. And I was quite excited about everything of which she was making me aware.

"Maria, do you think that before this great earthly calamity on the islands in the Pacific took place, people did not bother to intermingle with one another's clan, or family; rather they just stayed away, remained separate?"

"Nonsense! It was a beautiful society; no wars, minimum differences and no savagery. People were beautiful, Andrei, their natures genuine, and interest and love in opposites attract, intermingling is natural, inevitable for the human species; sometimes their relationships didn't work out, but they definitely intermingled."

"And us, Maria, two continents and too many years separated and away."

169

"True, my love, for we are its proof. It's the nature of the beast, his or her inquisitiveness. Slowly, over hundreds, thousands of years, filtering, spreading their pigmentation, their DNA throughout Northern Europe, Northern Russia—where the land was empty; however, the hunting and wild women, I imagine, were superb; then onto Greece, Rome and throughout many parts of Europe; also meeting other cultures of colors; man mixing, matching refining extensively, ideas and harmonies of thousands of years that for sure were practiced on MU, The Motherland of Man."

"Your ideas of intermingling sounds too lofty, Maria, more like, nosiness, individual kinkiness, or the erotic in us. And who is to say the latter itself is not an attraction; especially for those few exhibiting the sentient powers of their own inner self; those few exhibiting a fuller consciousness of the other is what makes us interesting to the other."

"As Diotima tells Socrates in Plato's SYMPOSIUM that some men are crazy for fame, and one of the reasons is that man wants offspring to have himself remembered for his deeds, if he has accomplished. Even if he has nothing of real merit, he wants children for their opportunity and his immortality."

"And, my dear, Maria, I imagine that was not the only overlying thought of making off with a beautiful maid at the trading ships; more like making out and then making away; if the planting germinates then oops, offspring. Honestly, I doubt if either was thinking of the beauty of his mate's soul and their goodness to possess, leading to earthly happiness and on to the divine; then, once again, who knows, for we were not present to witness their actions."

"But Andrei, those virtuous refinements to our world civilization came over time and much later, my love, with Thales, Socrates, Plato, Aristotle and those following them with new ideas."

"Yes, indeed, my dear, one step at a time."

"But my love, never were we birds of the same feather. We are people, tangible, permissive, real; we bleed; we die, yet marvelous individuals, forever curious, creative and imaginative, as those clever gods and goddess before us. Although the powers that be would love to keep us jailed as one common denominator neatly packed in one box like the TV, believing wholly its output; or on the computer—acting as one in everything we do, say and think because, truly, the powers that be are stupid and fear us."

"They do fear us; controlling us makes governing easier, Maria, even though today many believe we are the first to intermingle with cultures and races, and marry into human differences. And I agree with you, my dear, for we are people who are remotely trying to uncover our past and fight against the powers that be who want to keep us 'jailed,' as you so correctly say. But let me tell you of some of the stories I have been privy to in growing up in the Aegean area.

"Talking about mingling of the peoples, Maria; it's natural that I tell you that I am not true Greek but a composite of the many intermingled peoples of the Aegean. That entire area at the Eastern end of the Mediterranean Sea, from Palestine to Syria and inland are all intermingled blood—brothers and sisters—that came from the north, the south and the east; we are part of one and a little of something here and there; a composite of everyone and almost anyone. Both sides of the Mediterranean Sea all the way out past Gibraltar to Atlantis and beyond have been living, swapping and trading with one another forever, it seems.

"Stealing wives, pretty princesses and beautiful girls throughout history, my dear, is not something exclusive or unusual or unique, Maria; actually, quite common. Helen of Troy and Paris, I will tell you, are no way the first. Those two just got caught before the Trojan War, and they got a big-time review by Homer to make his lays a little friskier when singing them in the various households where Helen was related. Damaged goods, I don't think so; yet Homer has the Greek nation rally to beat up the terrible Trojans, rescuing their fair-skinned blue-eyed goddess. Let me tell you, my dear, you are right; it's part of being human. You are so right; I see it, but not as clearly as you, yet it does fit as simple as the right-size gloves. And there were no laws other than a King's want of arms and military equipment to give chase and capture the culprit."

"Oh, Andrei, this sounds exciting as we can look back, while at the same time the lady's abduction may have been wanted or completely unwanted."

"True, Maria, but how much more fun to call it what it is: the stealing of girls; or, as you say, in this case maybe not. The Persians scribes blame the Greeks and the Greek scribes say they are incorrect; so, choose your side because I believe each is right.

"Herodotus records that the Phoenicians came from somewhere East of Africa, perhaps from some coastal area on the far southwest side of India. Sailing about Africa, coming up the gigantic West Coast, for they had no luck in the Persian Gulf; perhaps the Red Sea, making their way laboriously through the Delta into the Mediterranean, I'm sure they may have gotten through, but it was an ordeal. It is said that they had already sailed around the world. So, why not continue once more going around Africa, exploring what they may have missed, and it is noted that they did record the sun setting on the Western waters—the Atlantic Ocean; nevertheless, they kept nosing around, for they were marvelous seafarers, following their ancient traditions. Keeping near to the coast, they sailed up its Western side and came into the Mediterranean Sea then continued as far eastward as they could, settling in what they claimed Phoenicia, about 2000 B.C., today modern Syria and Lebanon, however, I believe their arrival was much earlier; much farther back; perhaps as far back as three to four thousand B.C., or farther. And the tales of their social lives at home were quite diverse, exciting and provocative, not to forget promiscuous."

"Promiscuous? How so, my love?" Maria perked up with a wide-eyed sportive smile.

"While the men traded on the Mediterranean, the Black Sea, both sides of the Adriatic, into its many coves and corners, they brought home the money. The women were in charge of the house and ruled, especially in the playing rooms. It was quite a graceful and open society."

"I believe I'd like that if you were playing, my love."

"So would I, my dear. . . ."

"We digress, not that I don't love it with you, but tell me more about these traders, Andrei; the women they absconded with. I am sure the mariners departed hurriedly in order not to get arrested or chased; and, I imagine, in their case, sometimes the women were quite willing for the adventure of it. But that is hard for me to say, my love, I wasn't there."

"I love it, you're smiling, my dear. Everything was different, yet the spoken trading language was **Lingua Franka**; everyone who bought or sold things throughout the Mediterranean understood what each was talking about. It was their universal international language that only God knows its origins, telling us it's ancient."

"And I believe it was not impossible that that trading language went back many thousands of years. As they were traders, I could see that, my love."

"Indeed, my lady, they were traders, as were most such adventures.

Everything was still wide open, new and fresh. Venturing along the Mediterranean coast, eventually they arrived at Argo. Mooring the ship just off the sandy beaches, they began trading."

"You mean buying and selling."

"Yes, my dear, sales. At what are you laughing?"

"Nothing, my love, but I once heard my Greek instructor, Nicholas Merris, who was Greek with family still back in Greece, say that if you want to make things happen, 'sell something,' so how ancient is that?"

"How true, my dear; how right he is; it certainly makes the world go 'round."

"That it does, my love, even to today; furthermore, if sales were good word got around that they had some very good things to buy or trade."

"Soon, my lady, some of the aristocratic ladies and young girls came down to the seashore to see what was to be had. When the Phoenician sailors saw what loveliness passed, they became more attentive, friendlier. For these were very beautiful, remarkably outstanding women, appetizing; and, I'm sure, most likely, even though I wasn't there, their figures were marvelous, lively, frisky; and remember these were men far from the luxuries of home; furthermore, in that climate little was worn and much availability was displayed. So, you can believe that a little wantonness played out in the barter. Women being women; that is, inquisitive and very curious, in short, nosey; it is not impossible that they willingly accompanied the traders aboard just to see what else was at hand to barter or to complete the sale, fully knowing that the ship was to sail away for Greece, Egypt or Phoenicia or places unknown. And so, one day it happened that one of the young girls was Io, the King's daughter."

"Oh, my love, this is very interesting; I'm listening and imagining."

"Now according to Persian accounts, Maria, there is another story. This involves a Greek boat that sailed into Tyre, a Phoenician port, where it so happens that they stole the daughter Europa. And so, things continued to get out of hand.

"Another time, my lady, an armed merchant ship docked in the little port located in Colchis, an ancient town that is now the port city of Poti, Georgia, on the Black Sea. This was a little Milesian Greek settlement, established about six or seven hundred years B.C. Perhaps, this was an infrequent stop and a great trading opportunity available to all. During the excitement the little colony had all come down to the port. I'm sure that included households, the curious and, of course, all the lovely ladies with Medea, who was the attractive leader; not uncommon that she and her girlfriends were surrounded and helped aboard. Eventually, the buyers returned to their living quarters and the ship sailed away. Surprise, surprise, Medea and her court were on board."

"I see that you do agree with me, Andrei, and have some interesting tales to back up what you say; that at one time there were hardcore human actions, facts. For no one enacts these actions better than humans."

"Yes, Maria, and I am happy you are pleased, but what I find interesting is that these kings sent no representatives to demand reparation, and nothing was ever given. Maybe the King had a small army; or it was very early in the life of these settlements, with little to no protection."

"My love, perhaps these daughters were a big pain in the 'arse' to their fathers. Perhaps they were bored; that fits even today, you know. Finally their fathers and/or the King said, 'Okay, good riddance.'"

"Or maybe, Maria, the girls fell in love with their abductor or abductors and were content with one or just to be happy in a good man's household."

"So, Andrei, we concur that intermarriage was not uncommon, and bringing home a different lady made things more exciting, I am sure. Perhaps they truly fell in love; wanted and embraced change; or within some of those wild Phoenician swap parties, they met others and moved to another household."

"Anything was possible, my dear; and I am sure the boat with trading goods came more than once to some of these ports. Therefore, over time, getting to know intimately some of the ladies before a few were taken; perhaps she herself as others were captivated and craved a handsome trader's return."

"We don't know for sure, Andrei. Therefore, we cannot give the ladies or the traders a bad call because we were not there. Yet, the plot thickens, my love, and humans will be human."

"So, legends grow, my dear, creatively and exponentially, as they say."

"It certainly lent for exiting conversation, Andrei. Creative ballads for the families of the warriors who were, my love, gathered about the hearth; and imagination eager to create something that was out of the ordinary, coloring fond thoughts for the noble household. Definitely, it was food for exciting lives and good entertainment, of course, plenty of gossip that grew astonishing and self-sustaining to today."

"Here's something else, Maria. Nowhere is there any further documentation of the lives of these women. But it was quite early for these settlements, yet, much later, we do have stories of these women written in Greek plays: that Medea was a sorceress of Colchis (now an area in Western Georgia; today, Russian, known as Kolkhida). It was she who helped Jason acquire the Golden Fleece. So amazingly wild and fantastic are these stories; for sure, they were all real people, my dear. This is who we are today, still coming down the line of life; restless with new ideas, discoveries as are WWI, WWII; uncovered tales, written and hidden on both sides."

"How true, so right, my love."

"To continue, Maria, Paris did the same thing to Helen, but from what is written, she went willingly and was quite happy with him in Egypt, but their stay was short lived because some of his men betrayed him to the ruler of the area and, also, because the boat ran aground on a foreign shore the men on the ship were free men. Paris and Helen were betrayed and not given sanctuary; their whereabouts revealed; word was gotten to her husband, Menelaus, and she was returned."

"And what about the Trojan War? Please, Andrei, tell me it was not fought for Helen?"

"No way, Maria, no way, but it made a great story, creatively thought out and recorded by Homer in the form of lays. . . ."

"Which are short, lyrical songs; basically: lusty narrative poems, stories; ballads that were sung, and I'm quite sure, given the environment, often added colorful improvisations."

"To color matters, so as not to make them worse, Maria, Achilles was a brute, never a fair player; then again, it was war; hence, not to destroy his image, Homer made him marvelous—fair, upstanding. When in reality his myrmidons surrounded Hector and killed him. Of course, never trust a Greek suggesting a one-on-one combat, for we all know their gifts were devastating; their words meant nothing. It was victory gotten anyway, and in war that is all that counts, nothing heroic whereby the end justifies the means, nonsense; for the victors write history. Achilles took the glory of defeating Hector and dragging him about. Of course, his men were rewarded, for this was real human conflict, my dear, atrocities included. And give Homer credit for his creative portrayal and brilliant poetry; make no mistake, brilliant it is."

"True, you are right, his poetry is absolutely beautiful, my love. And it was Homer who gathered these stories from hearsay, wrote them down; put them into memory and behold what we have today, THE ILIAD AND THE ODYSSEY."

"Possible he had a big hand in the matter, Maria, gathering all the tales that were heard and still quite vivid in the memory of the following generations."

"And remember, Andrei, it was a big affair and a bigger victory with many memories and new variations now being created as I am sure there were other jongleurs."

"And his reward, Maria, was that he was welcomed into the houses of the victorious leaders; their family's prestige expanded; if it be a hundred to two hundred years later when Homer was spinning his tales of the mighty victory, so be it; remember Homer, too, had to make a living. And it is a valid tale, even if you believe the Trojan War was fought at the end of the Bronze Age, 1000 B.C. or 800 B.C., two hundred years into the Iron Age."

"And so, Andrei, some facts continue to grow, extending from the real to legend and eventually to mythology."

"But there is considerably more, Maria, and it deals with helpless Helen."

"Andrei, are you suggesting that it was Helen who started the Trojan War?"

"Absolutely not, my dear, but what an exciting twist to blame a woman; and, once more, it makes for a good tale, leading many of the beautiful women and not-so-beautiful to imagine that they, too, could cause a little war. And how clever is that to keep women on the Grecian pedestal.

"How noble are the stories of Greeks fighting for their women, my dear, and their great pain and suffering and loss."

"Andrei, another additive to the Noble Greeks is that they defeated Troy and all of Priam's fifty sons, especially after Paris broke all the codes of honor and virtue, stealing Helen while he was a guest in the house of her husband, Menelaus; then again, she may have willingly run away with handsome Paris; she may have thought the grass greener with the Trojan. And her decision we'll never know for sure. Oh, Andrei, I feel so sorry for Priam's wife, Hecuba."

"Not to worry, my dear, Priam had many concubines helping Hecuba."

"Case closed, my love, just imagining. . . ."

"But, Maria, it makes for a good tale and not one daughter to help cool a brother's temperament; all indicating that the mighty Greeks, no less, defeated Troy and her irascible fifty sons."

"Yet continues the defeat of Troy, my love, with Marlow's powerful blank verse lines:

Was this the face that launched a thousand ships?
And burnt the topless towers of Ilium
Sweet Helen make me immortal with a kiss.

"And yet Marlowe's beautiful blank verse keeps the sad story alive. Man, still, believing that it is Helen who brought havoc upon the poor Trojans."

"Poor Trojans nonsense, Maria; actually, the Greeks going up through the Hellespont to trade with the villages, and other communities on the Black Sea that surrounded the area, was prosperous; a great business was had on the northern shores of Asia: Turkey, on to Armenia, Georgia, back across to the west to Istanbul then back down, once more, through the Hellespont to Troy; this time to pay a toll to the Trojan gatekeeper to exit into the Aegean Sea and home with their loot. The Greeks were quite angered at all the toll charges they had to pay. Hence the Trojan War."

"In those days, as today, Andrei, it was the stronger that called the day and got free passage, benefits and privileges for being big in business or anything as is true today."

"Yes, it was, my dear. And the winners write the history. I know this is a silly question, but are you familiar with the story of the Hellespont, Maria?"

"Yes, the daughter of Athamas and Nephele whose daughter was Helle. She drowned in the river—the straits; thereafter known as the Hellespont, or the new name for the ancient one called the Dardanelles. They say the mother and father are gods, not unbelievable, but I believe they are real people because real people often name things after a loved one, especially if it were tragic, providing them strength to overcome their loss."

"Correct on the story, my dear, and I am beginning to see that they are real people as you are love's thrill."

"And thank you for that, my love."

"An entire basket of creative human activity metamorphosed into mythology, continued by the great people of the Aegean, who proudly gave it to the world. It is quite clear, Maria, just look at the examples of the man-gods: Poseidon and Zeus and yet many, many others; I assume a community. And yes, these people were wild, brutal and impulsive. Yet this Greek 'stuff' kept on giving with philosophy, sculpture, grammar, poetry, logic, mathematics, conversation, imagination. So, there you have it—humanity today."

"Then centuries later, Andrei, came the troubadours, albeit these guys were French and of the eleventh through the thirteenth centuries. Their forte was singing about courtly love, in most instances, an exaltation of the married lady; and these men of French song were welcomed into the houses of the leaders, or the well-to-do of the villages, telling the tales of love, and, at this time, Courtly Love was really big. Men would do anything for their beloved, even cutting off a finger or letting his beloved push him over while he stood on a ladder to plead to her his love at her second-story windowsill.

"But, Maria, it was the stories of Homer that gave initiative for this musical tale-telling career, promoting narrations, of how the household's great-great-grandfathers; sons' sons and of the many men who followed these now noble, marvelous warriors of yesteryear. So, imagination thrived, continued exaggeration and pride grew today's French myths."

"Andrei, my dearest love, I see there is a natural scholarship about you and a genuine curiosity for history. I like that; guaranteed, your life will never be dull, my love, for you are of a restless nature because you are harnessed within the confines of Communism. But you are not complacent; you want out. In comparison to you, I am idle."

"Hardly, my dear, for that is one of my great loves about you; you may be physically hampered, but your mind is a rage of excitement, full of ideas and comparative thinking, brilliant analysis—hardly idol. No, no, my lady, let it be known that you are my point man."

"And, so, still it is today, Andrei, in our modern world. Take some of our early American settlers on the East Coast whose butts were saved from starvation by the Native Americans who showed the tiny colony how to survive the brutal winters; eventually, with our greed and jealously for the land, we annihilated them; later the repeat on the Great Plains and to the West Coast."

"So true, my dear, examples are everywhere we turn, and not limited to the great wars of WWI and WWII.

"And the same was seen in the growing Government of America, my love. It was getting too big and no phones or cameras to record or to talk with someone when renegade settlers began to move in and take Indian land because it was there. In most cases, it was good grazing, fertile; good farming, good water, particularly in Illinois and Iowa; possibly, gold in some areas. Then, again, it was too tempting, too easy; no one around, few cared, greed won out and became a bad habit.

"Here's another, Andrei. Henry V of England, 1387-1422, invaded France; capturing cities and towns he was asked by the French King Mad Charles VI, 1380-1422, 'Why do you claim Normandy? It is not yours; it's French.' 'Because my men are all over it' was Henry's snotty reply. Nevertheless, six thousand English men with their long bows defeated thirty thousand of the finest of French Chivalry at the battle of Agincourt. Later that year, Henry married the nineteen-year-old Catherine of Valois."

"And once more the victor writes the rules, Maria."

"So, there you have it, my love."

"Oh, my Maria, you are a marvel, for I never knew you had such a wonderful background; truly you are my mentor."

"But, Andrei, I so want to be your sex kitten coming through the door flashing you, rather than immoveable, waiting wishfully for a miracle."

"Waiting seems too long for me too, my dear, even though I apply for a Green Card every year."

"Soon it will come; promise me never to give up, Andrei. Our time is now, the rest will blossom. Just promise me never to give up your goal of coming to America and pursuing your education."

"I promise, my darling, I promise, my love; goodnight."

"Goodnight, my love," as kissed fingers of loving palmers press to the screen.

*   *   *

The following morning, I awoke curious of what Maria had said some days earlier about seeing or making myself aware of the Native Americans in Arizona, the Navajo and Zuni, the Hopi. She mentioned something about a star. Then, when we talked again, she told me an interesting story about simple, natural enactment of an ancient religious ritual.

"Oh, Andrei, I was so excited being invited to such an event; it was a step back in history, all taking place in Blackfeet country on Archie St. Goddard's ranch. And I was witness to an ancient tradition. Truly the ol' West was being reenacted as it was a hundred years ago: cowboys on horseback roping calves, bleating objection, while Mother followed her little one down to the outer branding circle, where she waited for her darling to complete initiation.

"The calf was thrown on its side; one cowhand stretching its head another stretching its leg, making the animal immobile for its ceremony: ear markings or tags, hot fires, branding irons, singeing hair; for modern times medical inoculations and humane neutering. It was history repeated. All the families were there helping to prepare the meal afterwards, as the cowboys were finishing the week of branding over a thousand calves.

"While eating and conversing with Betsey and Talbot Jennings, she made me aware just to my left, under a big shady pine, that one of the young boys, about four years old, sniffling, holding back tears. His father, Sapoo, one of Archie's sons, put his arms around the young man, consoling him, asking just what was wrong and the boy told him. The father then took a stick, laying nearby, and drew out a circle about three feet in diameter; he then told the little guy to jump in, which he did. The father then told his son that this is the great circle of the Creator; it is full of protection and love. The circle represents the Creator's goodness and power, and life everlasting, always seen in the light of the sun, life itself, said the father, reassuringly; from the boy's reaction, he felt safe, comforted, even if he just thought of it. I was thrilled as was Betsey, who smiled approval, that such a wonderful symbol was so simply remembered and passed on.

"That's ancient, Andrei, ancient prehistory, part of the sacred symbols of MU from where these people came, over fifteen thousand years ago, landing by boat, walking to their HOME LAND, present-day Montana. All before the Rocky Mountains had risen."

"I admit, my dear, there is something substantial in it all; extraordinary how we are all connected."

And then I told her of my near-death experience when I was five. That it all began by being nosey; more like disobedient with a flare of curiosity, trying to impress my girlfriend.

"Sounds marvelous, Andrei," Maria smiled. "I'm all ears."

"We lived in an ugly five-story block apartment complex; my mother and her neighbor friend were downstairs in the basement doing laundry. The neighbor's daughter and I were about the same age, five. Anyway, she came upstairs to the third floor to play with me. Actually, we played a lot together in the local park with other friends and would swing each other on the big swings; you know the ones where the big kids could pump themselves way up and swing forever, it seemed."

"I certainly do."

"Well, this time we stayed in the apartment and began to nose around, and she began asking me what all these bottles under the bathroom sink were for. I told her I didn't know, and that my mother told me not to touch them because they were bad for me."

"'They can't all be bad. Why don't we try one; you know, drink some and see for ourselves.'

"'Oh, no, not me, that's wrong.'

"'You're afraid,' she teased again. 'I know you're afraid; come on, go ahead; you go first then I'll go next.'

"'No, that's wrong. I'm not supposed to.'

"'You're afraid, Andrei, I just know it.'

"'No, I'm not; here, give me one; I'll try it, I'll show you I'm not afraid.' And I did just that. To this day I don't remember anything, except that I was somewhere quiet, dark and no sound. All I saw were two funny people—I figured much later they were Angels. They were a man and a lady right above me all in white doing tricks and waving at me. They were very bright and very clear. Fortunately, living on the fifth floor was an intern, and he was on his way to the hospital. Coming down the stairs he saw my playmate crying in the hall; he asked her what was wrong. She brought him into the bathroom where he took my pulse and immediately carried me downstairs and told the ambulance driver, who lived in one of the downstairs apartments, quickly get me to the hospital."

"Lucky you!"

"You bet, but it wasn't over, Maria. When I was admitted to the emergency room and looked over, I was pronounced dead on arrival; when my mother came to see me, I was already covered with the white sheet; she was beside herself, crying.

"A few minutes later the doctor came in, pulled back the sheet, took my pulse and told my mother I was alive. He also told my mother that I may have been dead for a couple of minutes, upon admittance, but now I was alive.

"But Maria, most exciting of all was that I was kept company by two Angels; a man and a woman in regular everyday white street clothing; they were doing tricks, falling down backwards; then forward and waving and smiling, winking at me, swimming on top of each other. But the light around them was beautifully white, brightness I have never seen before; they were silly, and I do remember laughing. Just before I woke up—came back to life—they waved and told me: 'See you later; until then, be good, bye, bye.'"

"Have you seen them since?"

"Oh, yes, I have; every so often when things are going well or bad; there's no pattern, they just show up. Now for sure you think I'm a nutcase."

"No, I don't, my love, never. For I know Angels are here too; they may not be seen by everyone, but they are here, Andrei, I know."

"I agree, Maria; absolutely, I agree."

Maria then mentioned the Hopi who believed that some of their people came to them quite often from their faraway star; they traveled on an energetically supercharged pathway. Why not, I thought; like the speed of sun's light, which is slow compared to a prism's flashing colors; and if there be any delay in distance, the rainbow's coloring would hold some interest for the traveler; or, best, the speed of spiritual light, for is not the soul the spirit, the light of the Creator. And some people who have had near-death experiences go through a tunnel of some sort, ending where they are surrounded by the warmth of magnificent white light; they are talked to, often see family and friends, and they all want to stay; but are told they are not ready to stay; with disappointment, they return to Earth into their bodies, telling few to no one of their experience, but they are charged and completely believe in Life after Life.

"After MU collapsed, Andrei, many Native People made their way to America; much of their knowledge lost, especially how to survive without reverting to savagery. So, to help them regenerate, their neighbors and friends from their home star came to help," Maria continued, "as they touched Earth's soil, their bodies fully materialized, taking the form of real-live human beings. These people are called Kachinas; the Holy People, Angels, you might say, yet more complicated. They were related, relatives, to the families of those they came to instruct, spending much time showing their people—their neighbors—how to sustain themselves, regenerate the health of the land and to replenish the great loss of knowledge, human life, teachers, leaders, families and friends. Theirs was a good society, and the Kachina encouraged them not to lose hope but to gather themselves together once more; learning morals and values; planting crops, harvesting, building, cooking and many things about how to live a good life to be happy here on Earth. The value of water and its purity was stressed, for without it there cannot be life on Earth or anywhere; order, value and respect for the Earth, its soil, its wildlife and respect for other human inhabitants. Their instructions were simple, good. When completed their refresher course, the Kachina returned to their home star. Later the Natives created a simple religious ceremony to honor them, never to forget their help, to remember from whence they came.

"The Yei, of the Navajo, are another intelligence who are associated with the forces of Nature, Andrei. Think about it; this is ancient, my love, tying back to the very beginning. Perhaps 100 thousand years or earlier, when Man could harness Forces of Nature to help him build pyramids, Stonehenge, transport and raise the statuesque structures on Easter Island. It's all there, my love. Yet, I believe we have not totally lost those powerful ties to the Heavens because Man is marvelously brilliant, but content; lazy with now centuries of spiritual dummying down, using, at best, 3 percent of his brainpower. Andrei, don't you see, my love, Man can go both ways and return fully in tack. Near-death experiences is an example and proof.

"Then I ask, what about Jesus? Where there are records of him mingling with the people of India, studying in monasteries in Tibet, documenting His study of the teachings of Buddha; then spending twelve years in Himalayan monasteries in Nepal learning from the Naacal monks, the Sacred Inspired Writings of MU. Later you will see that I and my two doctor friends, the Stoddards, are another example of this experience."

"I think I know what you mean, my dear."

"I believe you do, my love; for they are with you too."

"Indeed, they are, my dear, occasionally, whenever."

"In the meantime, my love, leaders of the Native clans and their surrounding families were good examples to one another, to their youth.

Goodness thrived, relearned from thousands of years earlier; so, once again they handed down these perfectly remembered ideas, and Oral Tradition was tenaciously upheld: word for word, phrase for phrase, comma for comma as it was so learned or told so long ago; examples perfectly explained; for writing was not yet developed among the distant and isolated natives; everything was clearly delineated like a fine, delicate sand painting, a fine drawing, a meticulous weaving, a recipe, point for point; care of the Earth, care for each other; that's how goodness all grows, one step at a time as it was their form of human development. Not fancy, but it was their method, for some of the people were quite isolated. The result exquisite, enriched their lives. During this special time all was good; all was simple, and the people were happy.

"I remember reading of a court case in California concerning the Catholic Church wanting to raise one of their early Indian missionaries to Saint Hood. The tribe to which this missionary was assigned contested it, and through their recollection, Oral Tradition, via the Medicine Man, the case was quashed. Oral Tradition was upheld by the court as viable documentation.

"As time went on, Andrei, the clans grew into tribes and reenacted ceremonies honoring the instructions of the Kachina. To conceal their identity, masks were painted on the face, a mixture of flower coloring and animal fat; today concealment is quite elaborate, mask-making is more colorful, mystic, creatively fantastic and memorable; keeping their history front and center for all to see, and so it is today. So, guess what, my love?"

"Man and his family still don't see it."

"Correct, my love—he doesn't! Flaunting his stupidity, he calls this belief and ceremony a cult."

"Hardly, then again, Maria, man has lost 97 percent of his brain power, yet he knows everything."

"So true, Andrei; yet the stories are alive today, but no one on the outside recognizes it; they may attend a few of the ceremonies, if invited, but never put it together.

"Hidden secrets of the world, my dear, enacted right before us."

"Yet, these Natives, my love, as well as all humanity came from afar, gathered together to see if a great new society of humans can merge as Heaven on Earth. At the time the land mass was still connected, animals also came on these passageways too, eventually maneuvering to favorable pastures.

"Believe me, love, it is very possible that some Natives still hold secrets of their homeland, their star; for it took a lot of guts, a great deal of bravery to come from somewhere else, leaving all the comforts of home, to go somewhere new and become the people of today on this crazy planet. We are performers emerging from our clan or tribe, Andrei; now individual families instructing their children through home, schools, communities, churches—a continuous flow of education, education, education, trying to provide a better life here on Earth, preparing for our eventual return home. Then, maybe, next time, my love, to roam the universe at will."

"Maria, I remember reading that the Zuni were making silver jewelry five thousand years ago, true?"

"True. And you know that one of the main reasons the Spanish came to the New World was not to save souls, but to find gold, for the Swedish ship makers refused Spain any more credit; they wanted to be paid in gold for building their oak barks, no more credit. And the story goes that high in the mountains caves of South America, Spanish explorers uncovered gorgeous statues of gold; seeing that they were impossible to transport, they had everything melted down into ingots. Excuse me, my love, I divert from the entire ceremony of the Kachinas."

"That's what makes these classes so exciting, my dear."

"And it does make me think, Andrei, of Jesus when he, too, came to Earth born of a woman; grew up and began his public life, showing us how to be good and to achieve earthly happiness by first being good examples to ourselves then to others; finding happiness through our goodness here on Earth, and how that goes on to earthly pleasure: seeking the Father, preparing ourselves for our return to perpetual beauty and happiness, life everlasting."

"You think that Jesus read Plato's SYPOSIUM, my dear?"

"Possible, my love; Greek was still the language of intellectuals," as we broke concentration with hardy laughter at our intellectual smugness. "But I believe that many of these thoughts and ideas were given to Jesus, shown to him, by the Naacal Monks in India, an ancient organization as old as time itself. For this is the center of learning and Jesus' whereabouts from the age of 13 to 29. Later, this instruction enabled our Lord to preach, to tell to the people what he learned from the Monks: the simple religious doctrines of MU. Upon his return to Jerusalem, he told the Jews that it isn't an eye for an eye, but love and forgiveness, the ultimate virtues. That is the way of the New Faith, and this way is as old as time itself. Also how simple and helpful are the 10 Commandments which Moses condensed from Osiris' 42 questions, composed over 22 thousand years ago when Osiris came from Atlantis to Egypt and became the county's number-one religious teacher. These questions were to be asked and studied to bring Mankind closer to the Creator. It all fits, Andrei. You know it's not only similar to the Kachina coming to Earth, working with their families and neighbors then returning to their home, as Jesus did; the idea is the same. That is, teaching us how to be good which leads to happiness in our daily lives here on Earth and more so afterwards, where I believe there is life after life; so, this life might be called perfection time, ha, ha."

"That last sentence is very difficult to achieve, Maria, particularly your phrase: 'perfection time.' Now that's a ha, ha.'"

"So, did Jesus' teachings fail, Andrei?"

"Not really, my dear, but sometimes it fell into the wrong hands. For all, or most all religious followers, refer to Jesus as the greatest of all profits. And it's true. He is a human being and the Son of God; his life on Earth is confirmed at his birth by his family's enrollment into the Roman Empire, required by Caesar and by law. Yes, Constantine declared, on his deathbed, in 325 A.D. that all in the Roman Empire were now Christians. How's that for a windfall.

"Not long after this proclamation the young Church, in order to solidify its new authority, Maria, saw that free speech and independent thinking were to be quelled at all cost, for there was only one way now in the church. So, my dear, to solidify this Roman confirmation, the early Christians enforced the Roman-way. An example taken from the early Roman Empire: Where either you were with us or against; if you were against us, NOW the Christian Church, your soul was in jeopardy and condemned to suffer the eternal fires of the universe—a simple scare taken from the Egyptian High Priests to control their ragged populace. Christian Priests used this technique to convince ignorant citizens that the Church brings peace, salvation; to ensure this salvation, we are all to be led by men, for was not Jesus a man. So, MY DEAR, how's that FOR ANOTHER *CON OF MAN*.

"And such goodness, Maria, was not to be refused, albeit twisted, with a bit of pressure applied to help maintain the new religion on the right tract. Then about the 11th century A.D., the Church still continued growing in power, politics, and money, for they were the few who were educated—possessing land, gold and sundry riches beyond imagination. Therefore, it was deemed no more priestly marriages, all dissolved, withdrawn. Just like that eleven hundred years later, all marriages were void as Jesus was celibate. And not to be divided within families but now property of the Holy Catholic Apostolic Church. And Mary Magdalene, Jesus' wife conveniently rejected by 591 A.D."

"With a con like that it's hard to be good, Andrei?"

"Indeed, it is, Maria, and in this case Man's outrageous greed, his lust for power, control reveals, again *SO DARK THE CON OF MAN.*"

"As Socrates says, my love, in his dialogues in Plato's SYMPOSIUM (written 2500 years ago, and 500 B.C.), that with the concept of being good, one must first to thy own self be true. This is big-time serious stuff, Andrei. So, from where did Socrates, Plato, get this knowledge? Or is it just common-sense Aryan thinking, logic. And do you believe as does Karl Jung that one day all humanity will follow the example of the 'Holy Family.'"

"I confess, Maria, I'm biased. Socrates was truly a genius, and Plato in his genius put it all down."

"My love, I know of another *DARK CON OF MAN* you will find interesting."

"Maria, I believe that you have awakened me to many startling concealments."

This one is very interesting, Andrei, because in 1593 Shakespeare wrote his ROMEO AND JULIET based on his love for Juliet—who was very interested in the theatre."

"A true story, Maria?"

"Definitely, my love, and totally denied today; but my darling, my love, no man sits at a table in a hovel or in a writing room and writes such brilliant verse unless he is daily experiencing passionate love. No one wants to believe it because all the relative books and documents relating to the story are off the shelves, preserving the name of this family."

"And its name?"

"Wessex, my love. After all his is an ancient name, for, at this time, his clan was in England for almost a thousand years and the English insist that his name is tied to Alfred the Great."

"I imagine such house cleaning was quite an effort."

"My love, keeping all under wraps and noble society correctly preserved was a big job. All shady and revealing details locked away including those surrounding Elizabeth, the Queen of England."

"Fabulous, my dear, just fabulous, so where did you hear or find this information?"

"While sitting and talking with Talbot and Betsey Jennings, you know, when I had lunch at the St. Goddard branding in Heart Butte, Montana.

"And, Andrei, I have another link to the powers of the past, a contemporary one, my love. His name is Edward Leedskalnin, a gentleman in the 1920s who ended up living in Florida. Have you ever heard of him, Andrei?"

"Never have."

"Well, in my opinion he represents the power of the ancient rulers. You know, it was he who discovered—or I should say rediscovered—how to use magnetism and electrical force back in the 1920s to build his house, a Coral Castle in Florida City.

"Of course, he was threatened and roughed up by thugs hired by the U.S. government, but gave away no secrets. Later he moved his little castle to Homestead, Florida, where he conducted tours; and it stands today. His building of this magnificent little castle was verified by a neighbor lady, who saw him moving huge rocks through the air at night. There was some light, of course, albeit dim. But Andrei, many of these coral stones weighed more than nine tons, 18,000 pounds, and he knew how to interlock these stones as they did when building Machu Picchu, in Peru. Leedskalnin found the way how to use this energy force, and I believe this is how all these magnificent edifices on Easter Island were transported and raised; pyramids built throughout the Yucatan, South America, Asia and Egypt; the Sphinx, Stonehenge, and those marvelous buildings in Egypt, Greece and Rome. I know that I'm repeating myself, Andrei, but the parallels are just inexcusably obvious. I always knew that at night the High Priests were looking at more than just the beauty of their girlfriends; they knew how to use some of these techniques—these electrical energy pockets for their benefit. Believe me it has nothing to do with slaves pushing seven-ton rocks up a slide to build a pyramid."

"My dear, it is definitely possible that these people, who came from a star, may also had a means to apply this mind moving energy to build the pyramids, or by just sheer mental force they could harness this energy. I agree, my dear, no way did slaves on platforms move tons of rock up massive inclines; it's absolute nonsense! I believe most these things are meant to keep us in the dark; as part of *The Great Con of Man*."

"So right, my love. That MU was the Motherland of Man and those who came there came from a star; and I believe from different stars because we are all so different in thought, ideas, color, and language. And when I think of the great discoveries and ideas we have discussed, Andrei, there's no other way than to believe. True, stars are too numerous to count; they are into the billions and trillions and more, yet, today, man cannot imagine that he and other cultures came from them; it is silly how we limit ourselves, contain ourselves; put us into a box and are content to believe what anyone in authority tells us. True, snowflakes are perfect; yet stars are more perfect, and they don't melt away."

"Like you say, Maria: *'The secrets of the world are all hidden right before us all.'*"

"And the universe is infinite, growing, Andrei. For there is one God, the Creator, my love, so don't believe in the false gods. I might add our Native Americans respected the eagle because he flies the highest and closest to the Creator. The Eagle is associated with bravery, creative thinking, intelligence and independence. Today, we're too bright for all that; for we believe that we are gods, to a limited, hopefully imaginative extent, yes; in reality, no, never! But I do believe in people, for they can be terribly creative, exciting and resourceful, while some may be taken under the wing of the Creator, like Jesus and I believe, musically, Mozart."

"What about all these wonderful buildings, my dear, accomplishments down through the ages? What really is the Masonic Order, Maria?"

"A wonderful and preservative order, today badly abused; yet there is a lot of truth for what they stand for. But here's a contemporary beauty, ready, Andrei?"

"Ready, my lady."

"Claudius, a marvelous Roman Emperor about 53 A.D., not only led his troops to defeat the English tribes, but he kept a log of all his famous family's machinations. When discovered, by his wife, much later in his life—who I believe was his sister, although he did have a beautiful mistress-wife. Anyway, his sister-wife wanted him to burn his books because of the details he so beautifully recorded, would bring disgrace on their household, discrediting their family legacy.

"Being the scholar that he was, he would have none of it. So, Claudius went to the Delphic Oracle, a woman. The Oracle was connected to the Deities who told her to tell Claudius where to hide his literary works. The Oracle told him where his works would be in a safe place and not found for two thousand years. Eighteen hundred years later it was uncovered and 'I Claudius' was written by Robert Graves, published in 1934. A Heavenly connection? Or is it another *CON OF MAN*, Andrei?"

"Oh, indeed, and I know of the story, my dear, Robert Graves also wrote 'Belisarius' who lived not too far from my hometown, Sapareva Banya, in southwest Bulgaria. How marvelous is history, my lovely one? I just love it, for it keeps coming around and around until truthfully acknowledged."

"And what about the simple lines in the LORD'S PRAYER, Andrei, a phenomenal quest that I find unbelievably challenging, to the point of humorous impossibility because of our corrupt human nature: '**THY WILL BE DONE ON EARTH AS IT IS IN HEAVEN.**' Oh, my God, Andrei, this may be a reminder of how we lived on MU eons ago in peace, harmony, forgiveness and love; it may relate to our own Heaven on Earth. If there is a plan, we don't have a long way to go because it is all hidden right before us; in some cases, given to us, like Plato's SYMPOSIUM, especially beautiful when Socrates talks to Diotima; different thoughts of Creation, TIMAEUS; then CRITIAS and his recall: ORAL tradition. I know about these things, my love, I do, I just know. Please don't take me for a silly sick girl."

"Never, Maria!"

"Oh, Andrei, there is much more to tell you; so much more valuable proof that makes our conversations valid and your topical inquiry exciting. My love, I see things clearer to me now than ever before, believe me, my love."

"I believe you, my dear, I believe you are right."

"And the stories vary from Heaven to Earth. Not only from Greece; but from Asia, south and central; through Egypt, the Nordic Lands, and the Celtic world to the vast constellations of the sky as there are many. So, I ask, Andrei, who are these people? Believe me, they are not all figments of ancient imagination, although enhanced by them. They came from somewhere, and I believe the Hopi, Navajo, Zuni, Sioux and Blackfeet, way up North, may have some of the answers or at least a start.

"My love, when I substituted at the Grand Canyon one Christmas season, I was allowed access to the private collections department at the Museum of Northern Arizona because the curator attended one of my Washington, D.C., concerts. He knew me; and was very pleased with my Native American interest. But Andrei, my love, suddenly it was all before me, instantly overwhelmed, for I realized I was looking at a beauty. Symbols in paintings, on pottery, meticulously woven into rugs, clothing, shawls, blankets and jewelry, all were talking to me, telling me our origination—truly long before Greece, Egypt, Rome. The past contemporary yet all ancient; all before me; how long have these objects remained the same? What part of antiquity do these articles, symbols represent, depict; what do they mean; what do they say; what stories do they tell? How ancient is ancient for these designs, these revealing symbols, these coded words? It came upon me that this ancient antiquity is as old as life itself, and in my hands. My eyes see what our Native Hopis and Navajos and others of their acquaintance are telling the world. Yes, my love, I believe at one time Heaven was on Earth. Marvelous symbols tell us so, hidden yet right before us: the Soaring Eagle; The Forty-Two Questions; The Four Creative Forces, showing direction of the Earth's rotation, its winds; and most beautiful, most revealing of all: The Stairway to the Throne. These are but few. Eons later we have the Bible, Adam, Eve, Cain, Abel."

"And Man today, my dear."

"True, my love, but Man screwed it up; after all he was the Creator's image, not his likeness."

"Oh, Maria, these good stories help color dull lives, distinguish and enlighten cultural history, letting us know that we all have a long lineage of marvelous human entanglement."

"Oh, my love, how I wish you were here so that we could work together more closely. For you are my guide, my love; there is no one like you, and I need no drug to tell that."

"Or you here, my dear, for you are my lifeline, my hope, my example of success, determination."

Maria: "And you my pulse, my unfulfilled longing, my Prince."

Andrei: "Princess, you are my original work of art,"

Maria: "'Tis a game we play; this wishful pleading."

Andrei: "But you are my delightful little dish."

Maria: "How silly of me; I feel like I'm seventeen.
I'm free once more, although my body is still
held captive; not even good enough for ransom by
some desperate brigand. Nothing to look at or
idealize. Certainly, not a poster-child for
multiple sclerosis."

Andrei: "Truly, you are an individual, resourceful, while
displaying the living virtues of human
determination; its idealized symbol of spirit."

Maria: "Confidentially, I like being a Tasty Little
Dish much more."

Andrei: "Without you is distortion, that I cannot fathom
and never will; to miss you is unmanageable;
till next time I see you, Auf Wiedersehen. Our
eyes searching for next time say kiss me! And I
obey. Auf Wiedersehen."

Maria: "Auf Wiedersehen, my love."

*　　*　　*

Sometimes the drugs given to her make her feel that she is photographing her life on speed; she wants it all to stop, giving her a moment of peace, a wry semblance of happiness, from her tormenting condition.

*   *   *

About 10 P.M., Sofiya time, ten A.M. Seattle time, Andrei got a call from Maria's nurse-in-charge:

"Maria is dying, Andrei. She told me; that she wants no one in the room, neither friends nor family. (As you know, her mother and father have forsaken her because of her love for you.) And I obey her request; often I have heard you two conversing, and I have taken her dictations."

"Can she hear me? Can she talk?" I asked.

"She can hear, but response is getting dim; soon she will not be able to respond at all; she's breathing on her own; it's monitored. Her heartbeats are very slow and progressively slowing. Earlier, she has asked for you and gave us her directive; we honor it."

Sincerely, I had no idea of what to say or how to say anything. Never have I ever experienced such love and warmth; such simple wants and pleasures, and all sincerely returned. Never will I have or ever experience these same feelings again; they are all Maria's, and she has given them to me.

Four hours later, I still continued talking to her; response was nothing. Her nurse said that she was breathing ever so slowly; now less than fifteen beats per minute; yet slower and slower, and it was over. She was gone, but she was not alone. With her two Angels on either side ascending to gold, I knew who they were even before they waved back at me, Lawrence and Theresa Stoddard. Oh, my God, what love have I experienced; and what love awaits me.

Five months after Maria's leaving in November 2007, Andrei received his Green Card to America.

Eulogy

In return for such outstanding gifts to me and our family, I asked Maria to please send more photos of herself because I was working on an idea; in return, I increased our photo correspondence, but never relenting on our morning and evening conversations, that was just part of our family routine.

But I wanted to do something special for her that showed to the world that she was my love and no one dare try to take her from me. It had to be some one thing that said Maria the beautiful, the intelligent, the wonderfully talented, revealing her deep-loving personality that was only given to her. Then I saw it; a photo of her in three-quarter profile; it was wonderful, having all the qualities I so loved. So, I set the photograph on my easel and began to study it; then to paint it photographically with light touches trying to enhance all that I saw in her that was forever. My lessons with one William Neill, a one-time student of Ansel Adams, bore fruit, and the photo painting came out well. I sent it to the Multiple Sclerosis Center. Titled it Maria; AMOR, VIDA DE MI VIDA (Love, Life of my Life). They accepted it and printed it on the front cover of their quarterly: NARCOMS NOW.

A few weeks later, her nurse sent to me two of Maria's poems written a month before she left. For the rest of the weeks, I could not talk or work, pleading God for her safety. She went on from this world; but never is she gone from me.

Maria Poems

Soul

She's not fallen but found a way to rest
Makes ready to contend
Perfect, gentle on mark, smiles sweet her best
Prays God her last amend.

Whispers love then slowly she slips to gold.
Bright her soul ascends so joyful I see
Two Angels wait promise to set us free.
"I see all disbelief vanish, Andrei.

"What many cannot imagine, I see,
"Beyond all mystery is clear, my love.
"All blossoms and scent, it's verse and music
"Love and harmony ad infinitum."

She broke my heart then gathered its pieces,
Reading my soul made me forever hers.

For Maria,
Andrei

Maria to Andrei

In the state of grace since I last saw you;
Pray'd for you, thought of you, we fell away.
Married another, a mistake I rue;
My joy, relief: he said he cannot stay.

Peaceful nights, dreams of you, no denial;
To see, to talk, to feel our senses fire,
Kiss amorous, we snuggle and fondle;
Collective silence fulfills our desire.

Memory keen recalling that first kiss;
At my side, my favorite audience
Knowing where you are; never can dismiss
Vienna's romance, heart's madding substance.

No other's touch I know save yours to touch;
Never another heart that cares so much.

Love,
Your Maria

Andrei

Never my silence peaceful without you;
Gentle breeze my love recalls me to do.
When first we walk together how pleasant;
I so aware imagining's delight;
Senses quiver limbs incessant alert;
Emotions still for you never divert.

Watching you I saw how others admire;
Graceful movement that rouse hidden desire.
Near to me you sit; I mask false control;
Yet my heart is fire, for you love extol.
And now in earnest I'm to lose control.

Love,
Your Maria

Printed in the USA
CPSIA information can be obtained
at www.ICGtesting.com
LVHW050714271023
761610LV00002B/23